Reclaimed by Desire

Lust, Desire, and Love Trilogy (Book 3)

Desiree A. Cox

ISBN 10: 0692523316
ISBN 13: 978-0692523315

Published by Desiree A. Cox

Cover Art: Kellie Dennis at Book Cover by Design
www.bookcoverbydesign.co.uk

Editor: Melissa Gray Editing
www.melissagrayediting.com

Prologue

 *Jeff*

My heart raced faster than Usain Bolt's feet during the Olympics. My instincts were telling me something was wrong. Really wrong. I knew it. I could feel it. My chest tightened at the thought.

I had that all-too-familiar sting in my throat that had accompanied my feelings of unease in the past, and it wouldn't stop. I had a sinking feeling deep in my gut. I've only had those physical signs a few times, but they were spot on each time. And that fact scared the hell out of me.

There were some things that just weren't making any sense to me. I wasn't getting any replies to my texts. I had tried calling and calling, leaving message after message, but Nikki never picked up. And she never returned my calls. That wasn't like her. She may have missed my calls in the past, but she had always called me back. I knew something wasn't right. With each unanswered call, I hated that I was so far away from her and the kids.

Something had been really bugging her – it seemed to have taken over her thoughts for the past few weeks, ever since I returned to work, in fact – but she had assured me it was nothing for me to be concerned about. I suspected her knowing that my first trip after I got back to work had been with Blake was the source of her angst, but that had been over a month ago. I kept thinking there was no way she could be upset about that. Still, I knew she had a big problem with Blake, which I really didn't understand, since Blake meant nothing to me. She never really had. Ever since we went to the picnic at Blake's house, Nikki had acted very peculiar when Blake's name was mentioned. I could tell it bothered her just to hear her name. But I held out hope that having shared the fact that Blake was being transferred would put Nikki's mind at ease.

I had received some good news before going into our meeting that Friday morning. Super news. I couldn't wait to share it with Nikki when I first heard it because I knew she'd be ecstatic. It had been something she'd told me she'd hoped for on several occasions, for months, but that had to be pushed into the background. The only thing that mattered to me right now was finding out what was going on, and knowing she and the kids were okay.

I just needed to get home. I held the phone in my hand, listening to it ring and ring, only to go to her voicemail, again. *Damn it!* It had only been a day since I spoke to her, but it felt like an eternity. Not hearing from her was eating me alive.

The hours before Nikki stopped answering my calls kept replaying in my mind. I couldn't think of anything I might have done or said that would have caused her to be upset at me. When we spoke on Wednesday night, She had told me she planned to go to happy hour with her coworkers the next evening after work. We didn't disagree at all on that call. I didn't mind her going. We had a nice conversation. I thought it would be good for her to get out of the house for a couple of hours after work to socialize, especially since it had been a while since she had that time with them. We had Jessica still working for us, so the kids would be taken care of for those couple of hours. She assured me she'd only go out with everyone once a month, at most. I didn't see a problem with that. We couldn't isolate ourselves from our friends and I certainly never expected her to do that. Everything was perfectly fine from what I could tell.

Then I had talked to her earlier in the day on Thursday. Again, everything seemed fine. Our conversation had been cut short because I had a meeting, but it was always wonderful hearing her voice.

But when I called her on Thursday night, by the time she should have been home, I didn't get an answer. I had called a few more times, and left voicemails that clearly said how worried I was, and still got no answer. My last call that night was me frantically begging her to call me.

Friday morning I was a panicked mess when there still was no answer to my calls or texts. No one answered the house phone and she wasn't answering her work phone, either. I was so uptight by then that I hardly knew what to do with myself. By Friday afternoon, I had tried to call her mother, but she didn't answer either.

I was sick. Literally fucking sick. That was when I knew I needed to leave right then. I needed to get home. My mind was running rampant with concern. I couldn't concentrate on my own job. While we were at lunch, Sandy cornered me, and I knew I owed him an explanation, so I told him what was going on. Fortunately, Sandy was more than capable of handling things, and he and my manager told me to leave. I couldn't have been happier to have such understanding and compassionate people to work with.

I couldn't get on the plane fast enough. My thoughts had spiraled out of control. They were leading me down a bad path – every imaginable scenario raging through my head was bleaker than the previous. I tried desperately to trick my brain into thinking positive thoughts, but fuck if I could come up with one.

My heart raced with anxiety. Was she in the hospital? Had something happened to one of the kids? I'd like to think if something had happened to Alexander or Abby, she would have called me. If something had happened to Nikki, her mother knew my number. And bad news travels fast. *What could have possibly happened?*

While I paced in the airport at my gate, I tried to call her again, but all I got was her voicemail … a-fucking-gain. I took Tylenol for my excruciating headache that I knew wasn't going to go away until I was home and able to confirm everyone was okay. The blood was crashing through my veins harder than I'd ever felt. I could hear it rushing in my ears. My heart felt like it was thumping so hard it should have been visible through my shirt. A tingling radiated through my chest and body. One minute, I'd felt like I was going to hyperventilate, the next it felt difficult to take a breath without actually talking to myself, reminding myself to breathe. And I was drinking ginger ale, to settle my stomach. I hated ginger ale, but my gut was doing some massive flip-flops.

Jesus fucking Christ, just get me the fuck home.

Chapter 1

My breaths were drawn in as deep inhalations and I exhaled with loud sighs. The drive home from the airport seemed to be taking forever, while the pounding of my heart became more vigorous the closer I got to our house. I made each turn like I was a NASCAR driver. The wheels screeched as I made the final turn up into the driveway. I raced toward the house, slammed the car in park and yanked my keys from the ignition before charging toward the front door. After what seemed like for-fucking-ever to get home, I noticed the house appeared completely dark. There wasn't a light on anywhere that I could see. The house hadn't looked that empty and cold since before Nikki moved in.

"Come on, open up!" I said. I couldn't get the door unlocked fast enough.

"Nikki!" I called out to her as soon as I walked through the door. I hollered for her again after taking a couple more steps into the dark house, then I called for Jessica, but there was no reply. I walked through the house, flipped on light after light, and screamed Nikki's name. All I could hear was the echo of my own footsteps. The silence was excruciating.

Nikki, Jessica, and the kids were nowhere in the house.

I knew hollering out for her would yield no reply, but my heart couldn't accept what my mind was slowly coming to grips with. "Nikki!" I called out. My heart was pounding out of my chest as I ran up the back stairs, taking them two steps at a time, to our room. I was gasping for breath as I stood in the doorway. I could feel the blood thundering through my body. The room looked like it had been lightly ransacked. One of her drawers wasn't closed all the way, and a couple of her shirts were hanging over the top of the drawer. Clothes were strewn across the bed with some still on hangers, others were not. It wasn't like her to leave clothes all around.

I walked through the room to see if anything else had been disturbed or taken. Her jewelry was still in its place in and on her dresser. I fingered through it, taking a quick assessment, and realized nothing had been taken, or at least nothing that I could tell.

My search continued as I quickly moved into the bathroom. Everything seemed to be in place, and her robe was still hanging on the hook behind the door. When I walked out, I could smell the faint aroma of her body spray. When I looked down at her dressing table, I saw the lid to her bottle of lotion had not been put back on. That wasn't like her. I picked up the cap and bottle, then inhaled the scent before screwing the lid on tight.

I continued through the room to check the closet. "What the …?" I noticed the boxes that sat in front of the luggage had been set aside, and a couple of our suitcases were gone. That was when it hit me like a ton of bricks -- she had packed some of her things.

I quickly ran to the kids' room and noticed the drawers in the same state of disarray. Folded clothes had been taken from the drawers and set on top of the dressers. There were some of Abby's and Alexander's clothes lying on Abby's bed. She had to have packed up some of their things.

When I returned back downstairs and walked into the living room, I could see some of the toys were also gone. My heart sank, and I felt sicker than I ever had in life. *Why on earth would Nikki pack and leave without telling me?*

I ran my hand over my forehead, pushing my fingers back through my hair. *What was going on?*

I finally made my way into the kitchen and looked at the clock on the microwave; it was nine thirty. Then, as I turned to walk back toward the living room, I saw, lying on the breakfast bar, what looked like a note. As I walked closer, I saw Nikki's rings sitting on top of it like a paperweight. I could tell at a glance that the note was in her handwriting.

Jeff,

> *I'm so heartbroken right now. I fell so deeply in love with you, when I didn't think I'd ever find love*

again. I was gullible enough to believe you actually loved me, too.

I'm glad I was able to help you get what you wanted, but it seems like you won't be needing me any longer. I'm grateful I found out now instead of five years from now, but, trust me, it doesn't hurt any less to know I was being used.

The kids and I are no longer going to be a burden to you. If you want to see Alexander, I won't keep him from you.

I'm sorry I didn't stay to face you, but I couldn't bear hearing you say what I fear the most. I hope you have a good life!

"What in the hell is she talking about?" I asked myself out loud. I was having a hard time trying to piece together the puzzle, and found myself even more confused after reading her ridiculous words.

A range of emotions flooded through my psyche. I thought, *what the hell made her write a note like that?* I won't be needing her anymore? She was being used? She and the kids were a burden? When did I ever give her the impression any of that was true?

If I want to see Alexander? Why the hell would she think I wouldn't want to see Alexander? He was *my* son. I most definitely wanted to see my son every day! Was she planning to take him away from me? Or was she so presumptuous to think that because she left I'd no longer want to see him?

I hope you have a good life. She said, *I hope you have a good life.* Was she kidding me? What was she talking about? My good life was missing from the house.

She didn't even sign that stupid note.

I needed to talk to her. I needed to know what was going on. I called her again, and her voicemail picked up. "Nikki, baby." I rubbed my hand down my face. I was close to tears. "Jesus, baby, please call me. I really need to talk to you. This isn't funny. I just saw your note. If you wanted me to beg, I'm begging now. Baby, you have to tell me what's going on."

I read it a second and a third time, then I crumpled that piece of paper into a small ball and threw it as hard as I could across the room.

I could only guess someone must have said something to her that had upset her this much – I had no idea what happened. I was grasping at straws. I knew she wasn't here. And I knew suitcases were missing.

At least I knew she and the kids hadn't been kidnapped, and they weren't in the hospital. That was a good thing. They were safe, maybe. But where?

My mind was all over the place. I walked over to where the note lay crumpled on the floor next to the trash can. I picked it up, and smoothed it out as well as I could. I must have read that note at least ten more times, and each time I was more confused as to what the hell she was talking about. What the hell did she mean she was able to help me? Her words were cryptic and I didn't get it. I paced the floor like a caged animal. I rubbed my face one minute, cracked my knuckles the next, and scratched my scalp at other times. I was so frustrated I could have punched a hole in the fucking wall.

I knew it was late, but after trying to call Nikki so many times, to no avail, I only had two choices: call the police or call Rebekka. I chose to call Nikki's mom, first. I had to try to find out what the hell was going on. If she didn't know anything, I'd be forced to take more drastic measures.

"Rebekka, hi."

"Who is this?" she asked, as if she didn't know my voice or know it was me.

"It's Jeff," I said. I fought to keep the annoyance out of my tone.

"Hello, Jeff. It's rather late." Her words were clipped, and her tone was lackluster. She wasn't her normal self.

"I apologize for calling so late, but I really need your help," I said. When I explained that Nikki wasn't home and I had no idea what was going on, she made a sound like she was sucking her teeth. I pretended like I hadn't heard it and continued to tell her that when I had tried calling, I got no answer.

"You're going to need to talk to Nikki. I hate to cut you off, Jeff, but I have an appointment very early in the morning. I really need to get some sleep." I heard her yawn into the phone. *Fucking fuck!*

"I'm really worried about her, and the kids, Rebekka."

"Perhaps you can call tomorrow afternoon and we can discuss my daughter." *Why did she refer to her that way? She's* my *wife.* I wanted to talk to her. I needed to talk to *my* wife. All of this shit was driving me fucking nuts.

"Just tell me one thing, please. Is she okay?"

"Yes, she's as good as can be expected right now, given the circumstances."

What did that comment mean? "Thanks. I'll call tomorrow afternoon." I threw my shoe across the room.

I had to find out where Nikki was. I had to know what happened. Had someone said something to her? What did that note mean? What was going on?

I felt so overwhelmed by all of this. How would I find her? How could I get her back? How could I fix whatever went wrong? What could I do? What could I say? Where would I start? Who would tell me? I had so many questions, with no answers.

It was too late to do much of anything else that night. The one person I thought for sure could have helped, shooed me off the phone. If I started waking people up now, they'd never help me. And honestly, I had no idea who I'd call right now. I resigned myself to the fact that I wasn't going to make any headway until morning. I tried one more time to call Nikki, but was met with the same response -- none.

I stood near our bar and quickly downed two shots of Fireball, then refilled my glass. I remembered the night Nikki and I had been in that same room drinking Fireball. A hint of a smile appeared on my face at the memory. I remembered holding her drink above her head. Her smile was priceless. She tried so hard to stretch her arms up to get her glass. Then I had promised her a good fucking that night.

I wanted her here with me so bad. I shook my head as my eyes retreated to the floor. *Shit. Where was she? I'd give anything to see her right now. To hear her voice.*

I turned on the stereo, grabbed our photo off of the shelf, and then sat in the living room chair. Our wedding picture was in one hand and my drink in the other. "Where are you, baby?" I laid the picture down on my thigh and raked my fingers through my hair. *Fuck, fuck, fuck, fuck, fuck.*

I listened to the same song so many times that night that I had every word memorized. *These arms, long to hold you again.* There was a hole in my soul without her here. It was impossible to mask the pain, or to pretend I had no desire to see her. Smell her. Hear her voice. My eyes burned with unshed tears at the thought. Every sad word described the wreckage that my life had become. And over what?

I laid my head back on the chair, hoping to hold off the tears, but they eventually came anyway.

I dropped my head as my tears fell. I was able to wipe away most, others dripped on the rug between my feet. I was fucking destroyed.

I poured myself another drink, and again, picked up our wedding picture that I had set down by the bar. "I love you so much, Nikki. What happened? Where are you?" My fingers stroked down her shapely image. I looked at her eyes; she had been so happy on our wedding day. That day was perfect. *You made a promise to me, and you broke it,* I thought.

The only moment of my life that had been happier was the day my beautiful wife gave birth to Alexander, the baby I never thought I'd have.

The love gods had played the worst trick on me. They made me believe I had found someone, something special. *Well, fuck yourself, Cupid, or whatever you are! Motherfucker!*

I swallowed the remaining liquor in my glass. "Ahh." My face scrunched at the burning sensation in the back of my throat.

I set my glass on the floor beside the chair, clutched our picture to my chest, and leaned my head back with my eyes closed, and listened to my music.

When I woke up, it was daylight. I was still sitting in the chair, and still clutching our picture tightly to me. It felt like it was all I had.

I wasn't letting her go.

I wasn't giving up on what we had.

I had no idea what was going on, but I was hell-bent on getting some answers. I knew there really was only one person who could tell me where she was, and that was her mother. Whether she was going to say anything to me was another story, but I had to try.

Chapter 2

As I brushed my teeth, and while I had showered, my mind was fixated on one goal for the day. I needed to know the whereabouts of my wife.

I couldn't imagine life without Nikki. I didn't feel like I could live without her. She had captured my heart, but right now it felt like that very important vital organ had been ripped from my chest, thrown on the ground, and had the living shit stomped out of it. I couldn't even pretend that I could move on without her.

Ever.

She was everything to me. Everything that was wonderful.

I was hanging on by such a thin thread. Jesus Christ, my life had been reduced to rubble overnight, and I didn't have the first fucking clue why. I felt like I had taken a blow to the gut by a hydraulic crane that could level skyscrapers.

That morning, I knew I needed help. I needed some advice. I needed a woman's wisdom. I needed my mom.

It was difficult trying to explain to her what happened, because, honestly, I didn't know, but I told her everything I knew. I showed her the note, and she made that 'tsk, tsk' noise, and shook her head.

"You don't have any idea what she's talking about, Jeffrey?"

"Mom, I swear to you, I have no clue. I talked to her mom last night."

"And what did she tell you?"

"She said Nikki was doing as well as could be expected. I have no idea what that means."

"Tell me again, when did you talk to Nikki last?"

"Earlier in the afternoon on Thursday, before she went to happy hour with her coworkers."

"Well, whatever happened, it was at happy hour. And you can believe that it was bad. A woman won't just pick up and leave unless she found out something really devastating. Did you cheat on her, Son?"

"No, never. I'd never do that to her."

"That's good to hear. I'd be very disappointed if you had. And you can't think of anything at all that someone could have said about you?"

"Every time I mull this over, my mind draws a blank. I honestly have no idea."

"You're going to have to find out what happened. It's either that, or --"

I interrupted her sentence. "No, there is no or. I'm not entertaining an or, Mom. I'm never going to give up on us. I don't know what's going on, but I'm going to find out, and then I'll figure out a way to fix all of this. I want Nikki and the kids back in my life, where they belong. But I, at least, have to know what happened after we talked Thursday afternoon."

"Do you know any of her work friends?"

"Yes, but I don't know how to get in touch with them outside of work, and I wouldn't be able to go into her office until Monday at the earliest."

My mom walked over and rubbed my shoulder as I shook my head. I felt like I was close to unraveling. My eyes watered, and I was in a struggle to hold back the tears that were trying their damnedest to fall. And although I knew Mom wouldn't judge me for it, I really needed to keep my head together right now.

"You'll get this all worked out, Son. I just know it. It won't be easy. But remember, everything worth having, is worth fighting for." She leaned down and kissed the top of my head.

"Yeah." I was glad she felt so confident, but she was right, it wouldn't be easy.

My next stop was Rebekka's house. And I'd be lying if I said facing Nikki's mom didn't scare the fucking hell out of me.

****

I chickened out. I made a quick detour over to Sky's house before going to talk to Rebekka, hoping to avoid a face-to-face with a woman I knew disliked me.

I had mixed emotions regarding what I hoped to find out from him. On one hand, I wished that he knew something that would keep me from having to go deal with Nikki's mom. I thought he might be able to shed some light on this situation because of Abby. Maybe Nikki had told him where she was going with his daughter. Or maybe he had experienced something similar when they were married and knew where she might have gone.

On the other hand, I was anticipating Nikki had Abby with her, and was praying like hell she didn't tell Sky anything. I wanted to believe that she wouldn't confide in him about something going on in our personal relationship.

I rubbed my hand over my face, inhaled a deep breath before sighing, and then pressed the doorbell. Within seconds, Sky appeared to answer the door. When he saw me, his eyes narrowed, and he had a bewildered look on his face.

"Jeff. Hey. What brings you by?"

I shook my head in disbelief at this entire situation, and that I was actually getting ready to tell him. "You're not going to believe this, but I'm looking for Nikki."

"Why don't you come in?" I stepped over the threshold, into the living room.

"Baby, who is it?" Hope asked. She walked in from the kitchen, wiping her hands down her flowery apron. "Oh, hey, Jeff."

"Hi, Hope." I wanted to run. I felt like such a complete ass. What kind of husband doesn't know where his wife is? And what kind of husband asks the ex-husband about her? I couldn't believe I was standing in Sky's house, getting ready to tell him I had no idea where my wife was.

"Have a seat, man." Sky pointed at his sofa. I took a seat and sank down. Way down. "So you're looking for Nikki?"

It was odd being back in Nikki's old house. It seemed like it had been decades since I sat on her couch, waiting for her to come downstairs the night we went to Bern's Steakhouse.

"Yeah," I said. I dropped my head briefly, then lifted my eyes to meet his. Hope was standing behind Sky with her hand resting on his shoulder. I proceeded to tell them an abbreviated version of what happened. I left out a lot of details.

"Um, I haven't heard from her, but I'm kind of pissed to hear she ran off with Abby and didn't at least tell me. That's not cool," he replied. His tone of voice was calm, but his face had reddened.

"I was kind of hoping you had heard from her because of Abby. I was really hoping you could save me the trip to her mom's house," I said.

"Sorry I couldn't help."

"Does she have any friends out of town? Maybe there's someone she may have gone to stay with for the weekend until she cools down some?" Hope asked.

"Her friends are here in town. There's her brother, but I don't think she would have gone there. He has his hands full with his own kids."

"Ah, okay," Hope said. "I hope you find her and that everyone's okay."

"Thanks."

Sky stood and wrapped his arm around Hope's waist. "I hope everything works out. If you need anything, don't hesitate to give me a call." Sky gave me his cell phone number and shook my hand. Hope gave me a quick hug, and then I left.

It was time to face her mom. I was out of options. I drove over with a jack-hammering heartbeat and butterflies in my stomach. I would have loved nothing more than to talk to Rebekka over the phone, but I knew that wasn't going to cut it; I had to talk to her face-to-face. I was just hoping I wouldn't be met with too much resistance or anger. Hell, I was really hoping Nikki was at her mom's house. At least I'd know she was safe and the kids were okay. And I could see them. God, I just needed to see her, my beautiful Nikki.

My stomach had been in knots the entire drive over, but that paled in comparison to the feeling deep in my belly as I stood on her mother's front porch, getting ready to ring the doorbell. I shifted my weight from one foot to the other, shrugged my shoulders, and took in several deep breaths. I felt like a prizefighter getting ready to give it a go for the championship. "Ugh," I muttered. "Damn, Nikki. Why are you putting me through this? If this doesn't say love, I don't know what does." I raised my arm and extended my finger. My eyes closed so tight it felt like my entire face was scrunched in as I pressed the doorbell.

If Rebekka hadn't hated me before, I was pretty sure she did at that very moment. She knew about Blake when I dated her wacky friend, Gretchen, and I know she had to have said something to Nikki. *Fuck it, I couldn't let that cause me to back away now.* I needed my baby doll back. If her mom told me to swim across the bay and back before she agreed to tell me anything, I'd just be one swimming motherfucker.

My eyes had opened, and I hoped my face had resumed its normal appearance by the time her mom opened the door. Right after I asked her if Nikki was there, she made sure I knew exactly how disappointed she was with me. It seemed like she attacked me like a barracuda. Her teeth were gnashing, her tongue was fierce, and she was looking to draw blood. Well, maybe not quite that bad, but it was pretty close.

"Why don't you just leave her alone? Haven't you done enough? I know your past, and you don't need her. Go on and just live your playboy life," she said.

"That was my past, Rebekka, and I wasn't, nor have I ever been, a playboy. I love Nikki. Would you rather see your grandson grow up without his father?" Instead of focusing on her anger, I was trying to turn the conversation in my favor and diffuse the situation. That might have been easier if I had some idea what the situation was.

"I'd rather see my daughter happy. She hasn't been happy since she began dating you." *Ouch! That statement was the equivalent to a kick in the nuts.*

"That's not true and you know it. Nikki and I were very happy. Then something happened on Thursday night. I just need to find out what." *For fuck's sake, please, just tell me anything.* Where was Jim when I needed him?

"Rebekka, will you help me, please?"

I wanted to talk to Jessica. I knew she and Nikki had gotten close. She didn't have anywhere else to stay that we knew of. That led me to believe Jessica *might* be with Nikki.

"I won't betray Nikki's confidence -- surely you understand. She asked me not to say anything to you. My hands are tied, Jeff. Even if I wanted to tell you, I just couldn't do it." Her tone had softened. She sounded like she wished she hadn't promised Nikki to remain silent. "I will tell you this much, she's safe."

I exhaled my breath, relieved at her words. Nikki was safe. "I understand, I guess." I understood. I didn't like it, but

I understood. I'd expect my mom to do the same thing if I had put her in a similar position.

Feeling defeated, I asked Rebekka if Jessica and the kids were with Nikki or if they were with her. She told me the kids were asleep, but she didn't comment on Jessica's whereabouts. I had a very unsettled sense she wasn't telling me the truth, but there was no way I could prove it. I would have bet money on the fact that she wasn't being honest with me, though.

I felt more confident that my hunch that someone had told Nikki something was probably pretty accurate -- the question was what. There was no way that I could think of to find that out without finding Nikki and getting her to tell me what happened.

Beaten for the time being, I went back home. I called Connor on the drive and asked him to come over. I just couldn't take being in that house alone, and I needed to brainstorm a strategy with someone.

It was strange, before Nikki, I never would have imagined anyone living with me. I wanted to be in my house all by myself without anyone trying to impose their thoughts and ideas on me. But not anymore.

I had the stereo on, playing the same song from the night before. *These eyes, cry every night for you.* I felt like I was going out of my mind. I thought I was going to wear out the travertine tiles in the kitchen from all the pacing and walking around in circles.

How did we get into this situation? Was this really the result of Nikki going to a happy hour?

Connor arrived at my house about forty-five minutes later. Just before he arrived, I had managed to dig up a few more sad songs to listen to and changed the CD. None of which helped me in any way.

I did my best to explain to him what was going on. He was every bit as confused to hear Nikki had left. He kept shifting his eyes from me to the stereo and back to me.

"This music, really?" Connor raised his eyebrows at me when I handed him a beer.

"Whatever. You don't understand."

"Yeah, okay. I think I do, but this music is depressing to me." He took a long draw from the can. "But seriously, man, you don't have any idea what would have made her just pick up like that and leave?"

"No fucking clue."

"Did you cheat on her? And maybe she found out?"

"Hell no! I didn't cheat on her. You know I wouldn't do that shit to her. I love her, man."

He shrugged his shoulders at me. I wanted to punch him square in the fucking jaw for even asking me that shit. "And you have no idea where she might have gone?"

"I swear to Christ, Sherlock, if I had any idea at all, I'd be there right now."

"Have you thought about --?"

"Connor, that's fucking enough with the questions."

"Hey, man, I was gonna ask if you talked to Hunter."

"No, I haven't talked to him. Why would I? What's the point? He can't get me any closer to figuring this all out."

"You aren't thinking, dude. Did you forget who his girlfriend is? He dates Jackie. If anyone knows where Nikki is, you know she knows."

Without a bit of hesitation, I pulled my phone from my pocket and hit speed dial number seven.

Hunter answered the phone after three rings. "What's up, man?"

"Don't leave your house. I'm on my way over. I need your help."

Chapter 3

I can't believe I didn't think of checking with Hunter sooner. I drove way too fast on my way to his house. I banged on his door, rang the bell, and then banged some more.

He opened the door and gave me his death stare. "What the hell is wrong with you?" he asked. "Why are you trying to beat the door off the hinges?"

I ignored his questions. "Where's your girlfriend?"

"I'm not sure. She said she was going out of town for a few days. Why do you care where Jackie is?"

"I need you to find out for me."

"What's going on?"

"Nikki isn't at home; she was gone yesterday when I got home. And I think where ever she is, Jackie might be with her. And I'm ninety-nine percent positive Nikki has the kids with her."

"Wait, what do you mean Nikki isn't home? Are you serious? What's going on? What did you do?"

"I have no idea what happened. Everything was fine one minute and a freaking shit storm the next. Her ex has no idea where she is, and her mom won't tell me anything except that she's okay."

"You couldn't charm anything out of her mom?"

"No, there's no charming that woman. I was lucky to get away from her without any broken bones. But when I was talking to Connor, he brought up Jackie. I think Jackie knows where she is. I'd put money on that. They're together."

"That makes sense. She was really secretive and wouldn't tell me where she was going. She's not usually like that."

"You've got to try to get it out of her, somehow. I don't know … promise her you won't tell me – anything you have to do."

"I'll see what I can do, but you know how she can be. And you know how she probably feels about you right now, especially if she thinks you did or said something messed up to Nikki."

"I don't fucking care right now, Hunter. I'm desperate. I just need to find my wife."

I turned my head away. I couldn't let him see my eyes. I'm no punk, but my heart was crumbling more with each passing minute. I needed to see her, and feel her in my arms. I was lost without her.

"When was the last time you ate, Jeff? You look like a good meal may be in order."

"A couple of days ago. I'm not hungry, though. I don't want food. I just need my girl back. And then I want to find out who's responsible for all of this."

"Don't waste energy on an asshole. Let's go grab something to eat. You drive; I'll be on the phone persuading the pants off of Jackie, like always."

I yanked my keys out of my pocket and nodded for him to come on while he dialed her.

Once we got in the car, Hunter left a voicemail for Jackie to call him. He told her he loved her and missed her.

Within five minutes his phone rang. "Hey, Chipmunk. How's your trip?"

Chipmunk? Fucking gag me. He clicked on the speaker button so I could hear her side of the conversation. I wasn't sure if I was ready to hear all of their lovey-dovey banter and more chipmunk references.

"The trip is going pretty good, I guess. I've been spending some time out by the pool. I miss you, H."

"I miss you too. I'd give anything to be there with you, and holding you in my arms."

An idea popped into my head.

"I wish you were here too. But I'll be back home on Wednesday evening. We can see each other then."

I was sprouting ideas like a bean field. I whispered to Hunter, "Tell her you want to come see her, that all you need is for her to tell you where she is."

He shushed me and waved his hand in my face.

"Baby, what would you think about me flying out to see you? We can spend a couple of days together on a pre-honeymoon. We can practice for the real thing."

"Um, well…" she said. She was sure taking her time giving him an answer. "I really don't think that's a good idea, babe. Not for this trip."

He mouthed at me, "What now?"

I whispered back, "Keep trying." I couldn't believe he was asking me that. Of course the logical answer was keep trying.

"You aren't somewhere trying to replace me, are you? Woman, I'd die without you. I'm dying being away from you for the past couple of days."

"Don't be silly, H. There's no one who can take your place. Relax."

"I really would like to come see you. Damn, Jackie, I miss you, girl. Don't you miss me?"

"I do miss you. That was a silly question. You know this is just as hard for me to be away from you." She paused for a couple of seconds. "Let me call you back in a couple of minutes. Okay?"

"Yeah, that's fine, call me back. I'll be on the first plane to you if that's what you want."

"Of course that's what's I want, but this is a complicated situation. I'll talk to you in a few minutes."

"Okay, talk to you soon. I love you."

"I love you too." Hunter hung up.

I cracked up laughing. "You pussy-whipped bitch."

"I'm not afraid of my feelings or to express them; if you think that makes me pussy-whipped, so be it. At least my girl is talking to me."

My face heated with anger, embarrassment, and I felt a little self-pity creep in. I sat and stewed over his comments and tried to come up with some snappy response, but my mind was void of any form of wit. I could only think of one reply. "Fuck you." Hunter just laughed at me.

I drove the rest of the way to the restaurant in silence, hoping his phone would ring. We ordered, and our food came, then, after a couple bites, it rang, and *wife* popped up on the screen of his iPhone. *Wife? Seriously?*

"Yeah, baby?" He looked up from his plate at me and waggled his eyebrows.

She talked and talked, and he listened and listened. He didn't put the phone on speaker right away, so I watched him sit there and nod his head.

"I got it, Chipmunk." He lowered his eyes again. "Just hearing your voice has me coming apart, baby. I need you so bad." He ran his fingers through his hair. I'd like to think he hit speaker accidentally.

"I'll take care of you when you get here. I love you," she said.

"I love you, baby."

"Oh, babe, one last thing. And this is very important."

"Yeah, what's up?"

"Don't you dare tell Jeff where we are. Nikki's been really upset this whole time and she's cried for most of the time here. We finally got her calmed down enough that we can leave the room without her falling to pieces. The last thing she needs is to deal with him right now. She'll kill me if he finds out."

He hung up and raised his eyes to meet mine. He was the most lovesick puppy I had seen in a while.

"So they're in Las Vegas, staying at the New York-New York," Hunter said.

I couldn't help but be thankful Nikki was in a nice place that was in a busy area of the strip. And I was happy she hadn't gone somewhere like Circus-Circus. That end of the strip was older, and not as populated. I'd hate to think about Nikki and the kids out in the evening in that section. "Let's fly out tonight."

"Let's don't. We can go in the morning. We need a game plan, Ace. You can't just run up to her like some maniacal Neanderthal, toss her over your shoulder, and think things will be alright."

"That wasn't quite the approach I had planned, but go ahead, if you have a better idea, talk to me. I'm open to any suggestions you have."

"Jackie said they've been spending time out by the pool. We want to get there while they're relaxing. Maybe when they're enjoying a couple of drinks. That might help you."

"True, that makes sense."

"And, dude, she said Nikki's been crying a lot. I don't know about you, but that sounds like some really fucked up shit happened to her."

He sat there and stared at me. He was making me feel really uncomfortable.

Fuck me all the way to hell. It was all my fault. I had somehow destroyed my baby. Now I had to figure out how to patch her back up and make things right. I needed her to understand how much I love her. I'd give my life for her. I thought she knew that.

"I have to make this right, man. I mean, I can't live with myself if I don't do everything in my power to try to get her back."

"Then we should blow this joint and get packing. Make sure to bring your knee pads because I have a feeling you're going to be a begging motherfucker tomorrow."

"Ha-ha." I sarcastically quipped. I tossed my napkin onto my plate of uneaten food. "I'm so glad to hear you have jokes."

Hunter chuckled as he stood. I was so happy he had convinced Jackie to say where they were.

I dropped Hunter off at his house and told him I'd call later, after I booked our flights. He said I didn't need to pay for him, but he didn't get it. Without him and his girlfriend, I'd be spending another day in this lonely house wondering who to turn to and beg next. Fuck yeah, I was more than happy to pay for his ticket, and his room, too.

After I got everything set up, I called Hunter first, then Rebekka, and asked how the kids were. I figured I'd play her little game, if that's the way she wanted to be. I didn't want her to think I was making progress and had figured out she was misleading me. I knew if she had the kids, there was no reason for Jessica not to be there, too. And Jessica had nowhere else to stay right now. Rebekka's two plus two wasn't adding up to four. She was mad at me, but that wasn't my top concern right now. I tried hard not to be resentful that she had thought it was necessary to bring Blake into the equation, but that was my fault too, if I was going to be honest with myself.

I walked into an eerily silent house. Goddamn it! I missed Nikki so much. The house was dull without her here. I set my alarm, but was anxious and nervous. Knowing I would get to see her tomorrow, I didn't think I'd get any sleep. Hunter was going to come get me at five thirty in the morning. Our flight was at eight o'clock, our time, and it would have us landing in Sin City by one pm their time.

I stared at the wedding photo on top of her dresser. She was so beautiful.

I knew as soon as I laid eyes on her that I wanted her to be mine. Her perfect skin, her smile as bright as the sun, those big brown doe eyes, and her plump soft lips. I picked up the picture of her standing alone by the tree on our wedding day off of her dresser and laid it beside me on our bed, on her pillow.

My fingers stroked down the frame that held my baby. That dress looked amazing on her. "I miss you so much right now, Nikki."

The tears I had been fighting to stifle breached the boundary of my eyes and meandered down my face.

I lay on the bed and clutched the picture tight to my heart and sobbed like a fucking baby.

****

The alarm scared the crap out of me. I had no idea how long I actually slept, but it wasn't nearly enough. I woke fully clothed, still clutching the picture. My pillow was damp from my tears. Then it hit me, Hunter would be here in thirty-five minutes, and I needed to shower, and pack at least a couple changes of clothes.

My shower was as fast as running through a sprinkler. I'd have to take a real shower in Las Vegas. I grabbed some clothes, underwear, and my toiletries, throwing them all into a carry-on bag. If I needed anything else, I'd have to buy it there. No sooner did I get the bag zipped, the doorbell chimed. I scooped up my stuff and headed downstairs.

"Hey," was all that made its way through my vocal cords.

"You ready for this? I mean, really ready?"

"I couldn't be more ready, but I'm scared as shit, Hunter. What if she doesn't talk to me? What if she doesn't come back?"

"Hey," Hunter placed his hand on my shoulder, "she's coming back. She loves you. She just needs to know you love her and only her."

"With all my heart, man. With all my fucking heart."

"Grab your bag. We have to get going."

After the shuttle dropped us off, we ran through to the kiosk and checked in, then rushed to snake through the lengthy security line. Everything was going smoothly until I got pulled to the side for their gunpowder check of my hands.

"What was that all about?" Hunter asked me once I was found to be clean and let go.

"Fucking TSA. They're checking my hands for explosive residue. They did the same thing to me on our honeymoon." I shook my head. I was so close to breaking down, but couldn't allow that in this public place. Everything leading up to this moment was catching up with me. I took a deep breath, dropped my head into my open hands, and then exhaled through my fingers.

"Don't worry about it. They're probably just bored. They have to check someone." Hunter reached over and patted my shoulder. "Dude, we're going to get Nikki, just relax."

He was right, I needed to stay focused on getting Nikki. "As soon as we get closer to our gate, I need to get some coffee."

Chapter 4

By the time we boarded the plane I was wound as tight as a spring, and agitated as hell. I didn't want to stand in lines. I didn't want to wait for all of the airline stewardesses to take their sweet-assed time with boarding and getting everyone on the plane. And I didn't want to wait for the slow people to meander down the aisle at their leisurely pace.

"Come on," I mumbled. I wanted to yell at them all to get their shit together and get the fuck in their seats so we could get going. We sat in first-class and watched everyone shuffle their slow-moving bodies past us. *Just hurry up and put your bags in the overhead, and let's get going*, I thought.

I didn't feel remorse for any one of my bad-intentioned thoughts until a short, small-framed woman who looked to be about seventy-five years old stood next to my chair and looked down at me. She had the kindest eyes, and a smile on her face. She moved her hand from the seat back to my shoulder. "Whatever's bothering you, young man, it will work out. Just relax and have faith. Say a prayer."

I could only smile at her. A half-hearted, crooked smile.

"See that, even she knows you need to relax, and she doesn't even know the half of it. And say a prayer, will you?"

"Piss off, Hunter." And just like that, I was back to my pissy mood. "I just need to get there and see her. And I want to make sure Jessica and the kids are there, too, like I suspect. I'm not praying."

"Your anger is misplaced, dude. I've done everything to help you. Jackie is going to fucking *kill* me when she sees you. Do you even care that *you* might be the reason for *my* break-up?" Hunter ripped a magazine out of the seat pocket and flipped it open. He turned his head to face me and continued giving me the tongue lashing I knew I deserved. "I'm going out of my way to help you get your wife back and I'm probably going to lose the woman I love. So *you* can fucking piss off, man." He went back to flipping the pages so hard and fast, I was surprised they weren't ripping from the binding.

"Look, man, I'm sorry. I'm a douchebag, you know that. I appreciate everything you're doing. And I sure as hell hope you and Jackie stay together. I'd feel like shit if I was the reason for any problems with you two."

We sat in silence as I watched him reading an article about some wealthy couple's month-long vacation to Europe. I knew he didn't give a shit about the article, but I'd let him have his moment of silence. He'd cool down. We were going to be traveling for almost eight hours, including the plane change and layover we had. There was no way he wouldn't talk to me for that entire time.

The flight attendant walked through to see if we wanted anything. "Can I get you gentlemen anything before we take off?"

I already knew what I was getting. "Bacardi and Coke, please. On second thought, make it two." I really didn't care that it was before noon or that the stewardess looked at me like I'd grown a second head.

She looked past me, and over to Hunter, who was still acting all butt hurt. "Orange juice for me, please."

"I'll be right back." She smiled at us both and retreated in the direction she came from.

She returned a few minutes later with our drinks. I settled up the tab, and she moved on to the next row of seats.

"Don't sit there and drink yourself silly," Hunter said without moving his eyes from the Sky Mall shopping magazine. He was fucking desperate to not talk to me if he was looking through that thing.

"Yes, Daddy," I replied.

"You really are a dick."

"You love me, though." He just shook his head, but never raised his eyes from the magazine.

I mixed my first drink and gulped it down, then leaned my head against the seat. He was right. I was a dick. But that probably wasn't going to change on this flight.

I leaned forward and mixed my second drink. I sipped that one. The male flight attendant came through and collected the empty containers, then they all took their positions to go through the pre-flight spiel. A smile spread across my face as I thought about the movie, *Tommy Boy*, and the safety version done by Chris Farley and David Spade.

I looked over at Hunter. His eyes were closed, and his head was leaning against the window. He could sleep anywhere. He had always been like the whole time I knew him. I downed the rest of my drink, stuffed the plastic cup in the back pocket of the seat in front of me, and then closed my eyes.

I jumped when the plane felt like it was beginning to descend. My eyes popped open to see Hunter staring at me.

"What?" I asked.

"You're snoring, you tool."

"Fuck," I mumbled, then sat up straight. "Look. Hunter, I'm sorry, all right? I'm stressing here. Try to cut me a little slack. I'm a dick, I admit it, but I still shouldn't have told you to piss off."

"All right." Everything was back to normal between the two of us just that quick.

We switched planes and went through the boarding and pre-flight nonsense all over again. That leg of the flight was much shorter. It took less than two hours to land in Las Vegas. My heart was racing, and my palms became damp. In a matter of minutes, we would arrive at the New York-New York hotel.

The ride from the airport to the hotel was extraordinarily quiet. I think we both had numerous thoughts running through our minds. I know I sure did. The thought I couldn't shake was Nikki reacting really badly to seeing me. That would ruin me.

I drove up the hotel drive and pulled as close to the lobby door as I could get, where cars could temporarily park for check-in. We unloaded our bags, then I let the valet park the car.

My heart was pounding furiously. I could feel the vibrations radiating up into my throat and it felt like every drop of blood in my body was crashing into my head.

"I hope you're ready, my friend," Hunter said. His hand slapped against my back and made me jump.

"Ready as I'm ever going to be," I replied. "Ready as I'm ever going to be."

"Let's go. We'll head up to our rooms first. I'll text Jackie and let her know I'm here, then we can meet up and go find them."

"Sounds like a plan."

We got checked in and took the elevator upstairs. Our rooms were located on the same floor, with one room in between us.

Chapter 5

Jeff

I stared at my reflection. My mind was racing out of control. It felt surreal that I was here in Las Vegas for something other than a business trip.

My thoughts flashed back to the day I first saw Nikki at that restaurant. I had watched her as she walked to the restroom past Connor and me, then my eyes followed her when she walked back. I remembered the smirk that crossed my lips when I watched her rip that ponytail holder from her hair after she reached the table where her group was sitting. I had wished I was the one freeing her lengthy blonde tresses.

The jolt I felt when she walked up to me and introduced herself, and the palpitation in my loin when her skin touched mine for the first time as she shook my hand, were foreign to me. I remembered it all like it had just happened yesterday. I couldn't explain it, but I was drawn to her in an instant, and wanted her like I had wanted no other woman before. Connor was forced to be my acting wingman. Not because we planned it, but because I froze.

With a sigh, I pulled my cell phone from my pocket and sent a text to Sky. It felt weird letting him know what was going on with his ex-wife, but he was a good guy and was genuinely concerned. I owed it to him to let him know where

Nikki was. Despite what Rebekka was saying, I knew Abby was here with her. I knew Nikki well enough to know she wasn't going to leave the kids behind for someone else to watch. If we were going on vacation, like when we went on our honeymoon; that was completely different.

Jeff: *Hey man, In LV. Nikki's here.*

Sky: *What's she doing in LV?*

Jeff: *Soul searching, I guess. I haven't talked to her yet. I'll let you know how everything goes when we get back, but I wanted to just let you know.*

Sky: *Thanks, I appreciate it. Let me know if you need anything.*

Jeff: *Will do.*

Shaking my head, I turned on the water in the shower and, once it reached a little more than just lukewarm, I stepped in. I faced the faucets, while resting my hands on the shower wall, and let the water rain down on me. The powerful stream pounded against the back of my neck as I leaned my head forward. My tension was slowly lifted.

My thoughts went back to the night I picked Nikki up for our first real date at Bern's, and then our nightcap later at my house. That was a great night. She looked stunning when she walked down the stairs. The corners of my mouth turned up at the thought. It was funny when she told me the driveway was her neighbors. We had a great dinner, great conversation, and an even better time when we went back to my house.

Dating her, moving her in, and proposing had all seemed so natural, yet I toyed with her emotions. It was like a yo-yo, up and down, up and down. I knew deep in my heart the day we had talked about me not wanting children that I couldn't let her go no matter what, but I still didn't stop.

The rant over the pre-nuptial agreement had been another attempt to push her away. I didn't want to lose Nikki, but after proposing, I had gotten nervous at the thought of committing the rest of my life to one person – anyone, not just her. When I was on my way back home later that evening, I had a feeling of dread that she'd be gone. If she had left, I knew I would have deserved it. But she didn't leave. A couple days later, she signed the thing. She stayed with me even after I hollered at her like a lunatic.

I had fought my feelings that I knew, deep down, would never go away. My brain refused to accept what my heart felt on so many occasions. My own stubbornness was probably what finally pushed her away. I shook my head in disgust at my own behavior. I had no reason to act like I had, but I did. As I recollected those days, my feelings surfaced, and I felt the burn of tears welling inside my eyes, waiting to spill over.

I heard my phone ring. I took in a deep breath and sighed loudly, then turned off the water.

Frustrated that I was being pulled from my brief moment of reflection, I stepped out of the shower and dried off, then retrieved my phone as I wrapped the towel around my waist.

Hunter had really come through for me, but now my mind was second guessing my decision to chase Nikki down. I loved her, and I needed to talk to her, but maybe this wasn't the best idea. Maybe I should have let her have some space. If she refused to talk to me, it would shred my heart.

My heartbeat sped up while I listened to the voicemail Hunter had left for me: *Casanova, they're at the pool. I'll meet you down there in twenty minutes. Wait for me at the entryway, and we can walk over together.*

My stomach churned. *Well, I'm here now*, I thought. *For better or for worse.* I pulled my black khaki shorts and my gray Affliction shirt out of my bag, and finished getting dressed.

I stood at the entryway to the pool for a couple of minutes, scanning to see if I could spot them, while I waited for Hunter. I paced back and forth, then walked back inside the hotel. I had become impatient and wanted to just see her. I had no luck from where I was located because the pool area was packed with swimsuit-clad bodies. I decided to just stroll around, keeping my head on a swivel in case they got up.

"Hey there, handsome, I was just looking for you. Are you looking for someone special?" I was used to stares and seeing women talk to each other, but rarely had a woman approached me like this lady. She was nice-looking enough, but I wasn't available, and hoped not to ever be again.

"Uh, yeah, I am."

"Well you found her. Let's exchange numbers, and then we can get together later."

"No, thanks. I'm looking for my wife."

She made a noise that sounded like a whimpering puppy and walked away without another word.

Then I saw them. I felt the sweat pop up on my forehead and my back, and my muscles tightened in my entire body. I wanted to run to her and run away from her at the same time -- I was frozen in place, blood slamming through my veins and my heart thumping against my chest so hard it felt like it was damn near going to erupt from my body. *God damn it, how did it get to this?*

I took another couple of steps. The spider senses in Jackie must have felt my foot take that last step closer to their lounge chairs because her head popped up, snapping in my direction as she looked directly at me, causing me to stop on a dime. My breath caught in my throat. My body stiffened. Her eyes had me glued in my position. I saw her mouth moving, then Nikki lifted her beautiful head and looked around until our eyes locked.

I was committed to the reason I was here, and I just couldn't wait any longer for Hunter. I was met by Jackie's slender frame blocking the path to get to my wife. "Excuse me, Jackie." I opted to be polite in case this little pit bull decided to unleash on me.

"What the hell are you doing here?"

"Jackie, please, this doesn't concern you. I just need to talk to Nikki." I had to restrain myself from flipping out on her. Even though I had expected it, I didn't need her mouthiness. I was already on edge. "Nikki --" I was interrupted by another dose of Jackie's venom.

"Like hell it doesn't. Nikki's like a sister to me. I think you've totally done enough damage." She widened her stance and lodged her small fists at her hips. "Don't you get it? She's done with you; you've pushed her clean off the proverbial edge. That's why she left."

"Seriously, I'm just asking you to give me a minute with my wife, please." She wasn't making this easy. The thought crossed my mind to just pick her up and set her off to the side, but I restrained myself.

"You made a mockery of your marriage, and now, now, after all of this …"

"Jackie." Her head turned, and she was practically face-to-face with Hunter. "Zip it, babe, and come with me. Let them talk." It was about time he got out here with me. Of course, I probably should have waited for him like he had told me to. I was so glad Hunter had to come with me so he could run interference with his girlfriend.

"What the hell, Hunter? I told you not to do this!" she screamed. "How could you?"

"Please, just come with me." How he was able to stay so calm was beyond me, but I needed to learn how to do that.

After a short, heated protest, Jackie reluctantly left with Hunter, but not before calling me an asshole, not so under her breath. Hunter put his arm around her shoulder, steering her toward the other side of the pool as her hands flailed about, gesturing her unhappiness and protest. I'm pretty sure I got flipped off. I loved that Jackie cared for Nikki, but she had no idea how much I loved this woman. Unfortunately, I didn't think Nikki really knew either.

Nikki pushed her sunglasses on top of her head, then glared up at me with tear-filled eyes. "I've got nothing to say to you, Jeff. Not right now." The fact that I was responsible for her obvious distress made me feel like hot, fresh dog shit. No matter what happened, she didn't deserve to feel that devastated.

"Nikki, please, just talk to me for five minutes," I said. "Please, baby, I'm begging you."

"I just can't do this, Jeff." A tear trickled down her face. I wanted to wipe it, or kiss it away. I wanted to pull her up from the chair into me and hold her, never letting her go. But somehow, some-unknown-fucking-how, I had become such an ass in her opinion, that I knew she wouldn't let me touch her right now. I was near crumbling, seeing this beautiful, broken woman, my wife, in front of me.

"Jesus, Nikki, I --" I choked on my own words. I didn't even know what I wanted to say. I'm sorry wasn't going to be enough, and I didn't even know what I was supposed to apologize for. Saying "I love you" would probably just be empty words right now to her. I knew I did love her, but she didn't. I could see it in her eyes. I had to find a way to explain myself to her, and I needed her to tell me what was going on. But how? I sat down on the lounge chair Jackie had occupied.

"How did you find me?" She sat up and crossed her arms over her chest.

"I begged and pleaded with everyone to tell me where you were. I even begged your mom to tell me anything. I need you, baby doll. I can't live without you."

She flipped her sunglasses back down to cover her eyes. "Go tell it to Blake." The tears were streaming down her face; drips fell from her chin, landing on her arms. "Did you call her baby doll too?" She swiped at her tears. "My mom warned me about you, but I wouldn't listen. I thought …" She rubbed her hands over her cheeks, wiping the tears away again.

"You thought what? And why would you mention Blake? She's nothing to me. She never has been. This is between us; you're the one I love."

She laughed. It was pretty messed up that she took a brief break from crying to laugh at me pouring my heart out to her. I guess, maybe, I deserved her skepticism. I didn't understand how, but I also didn't know what made her flee in the first place.

"But seriously, Jeff, what do you want from me? I'm so drained emotionally right now, maybe we just need to put an end to this and move on." Her face and mouth scrunched up as round two of the tear-flood began. She looked away toward the other side of the pool.

"Is that what *you* really want? Don't shut me out, baby doll. Please." I reached to take her hand in mine, but she pulled hers back and tucked it under her thigh.

Her sobs got more vocal. It was only a matter of time before I would be in tears too. I couldn't lose her. I may as well be dead if she wasn't going to be in my life.

Chapter 6

 Nikki

I felt like everyone was staring at us. "I can't do this here." My voice was barely audible as I managed to choke those few words out of my tightened throat. I wanted to run. I wanted something or someone to distract him so I could take off running to the elevator and hide in my room.

My emotions had been all over the place. I bounced from heart-break to anger and then back again. Jessica was with me most of the time, so I felt pretty confident that she hadn't been the one to say anything to Jeff, but she had gone to dinner with that guy she met. My mom promised me she wouldn't say anything, and I didn't think she would be responsible for Jeff being in Las Vegas. And Jackie knew I didn't want him here. She knew I wasn't ready to talk to him, yet here he was. I never said anything to Sky. In retrospect, I probably should have at least let him know I was going to be out of town, but I didn't want to drag him into this mess. I didn't completely understand why, but my gut feeling was telling me it was Jackie who blabbed to Hunter where we were. *What the hell could he have said to convince her it was all right to tell him? I didn't even realize they were that close of friends.*

Now, I was forced to contend with Jeff. That really pissed me off because I wasn't positive that I was ready to have the difficult conversation with him that we needed to have, not yet. I just wanted some time to think things through and figure out how I was going to approach this when I got back. I stood and grabbed my towel, wrapping it around my body as I slipped on my flip-flops. I just wanted to leave.

"When, then? Please, don't just walk away from me," Jeff asked. "Why not let me take you to dinner tonight? We can sit down in public and talk then."

"I don't know. I ..." I swallowed hard. "I ..." The tears continued to flow down my face, and I couldn't even get my sentence out.

"Let's meet in the lobby at seven. Is that okay? Just take that one step, baby, please?"

I looked around at the people sitting nearby. As I suspected, they were staring at us. They were hanging on his pleading questions, awaiting my replies. My heart was saying go talk to him, go at least listen to his side of the story. I wanted so badly to follow my heart. But there was a sense of impending doom that shouted, *No, don't do it!* All of the thoughts in my head were causing pure chaos, but I knew deep down, I owed him at least a chance to explain himself. And as much as I cringed at the thought of being forced to do this now, it may as well be tonight, since he was here. "Okay."

He let out his breath in a huge sigh that sounded as if he had been holding it for five minutes. "Thank you, Nikki." His hand reached out to me, and I turned to avoid his touch. I felt terrible for it. That was the second time he had tried to make contact with me, and I had shunned both attempts. "How are the kids? Alexander, is he okay?"

"The kids are fine. Alexander's good. They're here with me, but you probably knew that already. Jessica is watching them right now."

"I really *need* to see them, Nikki." I could hear the desperation in his voice. I had expected he'd be pissed, especially that I had taken his son.

"I guess you can come up and see them now. Please, just don't be upset with me. I wasn't trying to make you mad, Jeff, but I couldn't leave them at home, obviously." I reached out, touched his arm, and felt need surge through me. I had known that would happen. With my fingers still on his skin, my eyes closed for a few seconds, and I inhaled deeply before releasing my breath and fixing my gaze on him. The look of disappointment that had flashed on his face dissipated, and I pulled my hand back.

At that moment, I wanted so badly for Jeff to wrap his arms around me and hold me tight against his chest. I wanted him to inhale my scent like he had done so many times in the past. I was aching for him to show me a sign, any sign, that he truly loved me.

But if he had done that, and if I had let him in, I knew I'd never get the answers to the questions I needed to ask. I don't think I would've been able to find the strength to even ask the tough questions about what Jason had told me. I had to know if he was out of town with Blake, if he had lied to me about being with Sandy. And I had to know if he married me just to get that promotion. And I needed to know if he still had feelings for Blake. The thought of any of the things Jason said being true made me sick to my stomach.

I turned and began walking and I could see his shadow following me.

 Jeff

Begging wasn't beneath me. I wasn't afraid to ask, or beg, to see her later that night.

Rebekka hadn't told me the truth, but I wasn't surprised to confirm that. I had already been suspicious of her telling me the kids were there with her. I didn't blame her. I knew she was saying what Nikki had asked her to.

I felt anger taking over at the thought that Nikki had uprooted the kids and taken my son from me to have a hissy-fit over who fucking knows what. Then, like magic, her touch soothed my irritation. My cock jerked. I ached to feel her hands on more of me. I loved the feel of her caress. And I was relieved after she pulled away from me twice, even if it was just a quick stroke of my arm. I watched her expression, and I could tell she felt a reconnect when her hand landed on me.

Nikki turned to walk back toward the hotel entrance. Before I followed her, I turned my head over toward the side of the pool where Hunter and Jackie were. She had her back to me, sitting on a stool at the bar, while Hunter stood beside her, his arm snaked around her waist. He glanced up, like he could sense me looking in their direction, and gave me a subtle thumbs-up behind Jackie's back. With a quick nod, I returned my attention to following Nikki to go see my babies.

Abby may not have been mine by blood, but she lived with me and I loved her. She'd be treated like she was mine. I'd never do anything that was disrespectful to Sky, but I needed him to trust me, and to always know that I'd have Abby's best interests at heart while caring for her.

We reached Nikki's room, and she hesitated for a moment before sliding the key card to open the door. She stopped and turned to me before opening the door all the way. "You can only be here for a few minutes right now, but we can meet up another time for you to see Alexander again. Is that okay?" Her eyes were wet. She was struggling to hold the tears at bay, but they were on the verge of falling.

"I didn't come up here to upset you, or only to see Alexander, Nikki. I came to see Abby, too. I won't stay longer than you're comfortable with, for now." The tears toppled down her face. I couldn't wait to get her alone later to try to understand what made absolutely no sense to me.

She wiped at her face as she pushed the door open. When we walked in, Abby came running toward her. "Mommy." My heart shattered. She was really going to take everything away from me without even talking to me?

Jessica looked at me like she was staring at a ghost. "Hi, Jessica."

"Um, Jeff, hi," she said. Her mouth was agape.

Abby stepped around Nikki and looked at me. "Daddy Jeff," she whispered. We had agreed that was how Abby would refer to me. We made sure Sky was okay with it, because he was Daddy. We all agreed that we thought it would help to make sure she understood my role as she got older. I wasn't Uncle Jeff, I wasn't Cousin Jeff, I was Daddy Jeff.

I knelt down and held my arms open to catch her as she lunged toward me. I stood and held her tight. I had been clueless about how much joy kids could bring a person. How much they make things that aren't right, right. They're so innocent and forgiving. I may never have known this feeling if it hadn't been for my beautiful Nikki. I was learning a lot from her.

After talking with Abby, getting her highlights about being on the flight to Las Vegas, and her thoughts on the hotel and pool, she darted off to Jessica, who was holding my Alexander. He was sound asleep.

I walked over to take him, and she stood, like she had done so many times before, to make the transfer from her arms to mine a little easier, and hopefully less disruptive. Once I had him securely in my arms, his head rested on my shoulder, I exhaled the breath I had been holding. My son, my little man. He was back with me where he belonged. Holding him felt so perfect.

I walked over to the window while rubbing his back. There was no mistaking that he was eating well. He had put on a good amount of weight since his birth. I stared out the window at nothing in particular as I fought to keep my emotions under control. I never wanted to leave. I never wanted Nikki to leave. We were supposed to be together. We were a family.

I lowered my gaze to look at his peaceful, perfect face, his little lips crooked as he slept. Lucky him, he had no idea what was going on. *Don't worry, little man, I'll get this all figured out and fixed so you never need to be away from me again*, I thought. My little guy inhaled and sighed, and his little fingers rubbed and grabbed at my neck. It was as if he could read my thoughts. He knew he was safe in my arms.

"Jeff," Nikki whispered. Her eye were reddened and she looked tired. "Jeff, let me take him and get him laid down so he stays asleep."

"Fine." That wasn't what I was thinking, but that was the response I settled on. I wanted to stay and hold my son until he woke, but I didn't want to upset Nikki any more than she already was.

After getting Alexander in the crib, she placed her hand on my lower back to coax me to move toward the door. "We'll see each other later," she said.

"Nikki, please don't stand me up."

"I won't. I promise. I'll be downstairs at seven o'clock sharp."

Chapter 7

As soon as the door clicked shut behind him, I turned back to face into the room, and sighed. I leaned my back and head against the door. Somehow, I had to get it together so Abby didn't see me an emotional, teary-eyed wreck again. I walked back into the room.

"That was a shock to see Jeff here. How do you think he found you?"

"I think I know, and it really pisses me off. I talked to my mother after he went by her house, and she swore to me she didn't tell him anything. If you didn't tell him, there's only one other person," I replied. I walked over to the chair beside where Jessica was lying on the bed with Abby beside her. "Jackie. She must have told Hunter, and well, guess who Hunter told?"

"I didn't say anything. Why would she do that to you?"

"That's a good question. She's still down at the pool with Hunter. He showed up and whisked her away so we could talk after Jeff appeared out of nowhere." I used my fingers to make air quotes when I said talk. "You can believe that I'll be asking her that exact question."

"Did I hear you say you're meeting with Jeff later?"

"Yeah. You don't mind watching the kids tonight, do you?"

"Of course not. You have to get this talked out. You owe him that, Nikki. He deserves to know what's going on."

"What's going on, Mommy?" Abby twisted her body so she could face me.

"Nothing for you to be concerned about, my dear little baby girl. Everything is just fine. Watch your show."

"When are we going home? I miss my room and *my* babies." Her lower lip poked out as she pouted.

"In a couple of days. When our vacation is over, Abby, then we'll go back home to see your babies."

"Okay," she replied. She lay flat on her stomach and resumed watching cartoons.

I lowered my shaking head into my hands and massaged my temples. I was exhausted. I had known I'd have to face him. I just hadn't expected it to be for another couple of days. "I won't be out long," I muttered.

Jeff

I stared at myself in the mirror above the desk in my room while shaking my head. The whole situation was pretty fucking ridiculous. I had to take time off from work, fly out to Las Vegas, convince my wife to even talk to me, convince her to let me see the kids, convince her to go to dinner with me, just so I could try like fuck to convince her to tell me what the hell was going on, and eventually come home. *What the fuck did it all mean?* Whatever I had to do, I'd do it. I wasn't planning to leave Las Vegas alone. I just hoped she recognized how much I was jumping through hoops for her.

I hoisted my bag up onto the bed and pulled out the clothes I had jammed into it. I had just finished hanging them up, my thoughts running rampant, when I heard a knock on my door.

I looked through the peephole, but saw no one. "Who is it?"

"It's me. Open up," Hunter said.

My eyes rolled as I remembered Jackie playing guard dog down by the pool, then I pulled open the door. "What's up? Did you get your girlfriend calmed down?"

"Yeah, man, she's cool." He stepped inside the room, and I closed the door. "I came up here to tell you what she just told me. You need to hear this, but you're going to need to sit down first."

We made our way over to the table and chairs near the window. "All right, tell me."

The more Hunter talked, the higher it felt like my blood pressure was rising. I began to sweat, and I could feel my chest tighten. It became increasingly more difficult to breathe. It felt like the pressure in my head was going to cause an explosion and the top of my skull was going to blow clean off my body. My muscles tensed, and my jaw clenched so tight I was surprised I didn't break any teeth. I flexed my fingers one minute and balled my fist so tight my knuckles turned white the next. I could have killed someone. I wasn't on any blood pressure medicine, but at this rate, I'd need to be, and soon.

"Stop!" I screamed. I stood from the chair, pushing it back hard enough that it fell onto its side. "Stop talking or I'm going to fucking lose my mind." I paced the room taking deep breaths and exhaling through my mouth in an attempt to regain my composure.

"Calm down, man. Now that you heard this, just imagine how Nikki must have felt that night in the bar."

"That piece of shit! Jason will pay for this shit. Motherfuck!" I was back to pacing. It felt like the walls of the room were closing in on me. It was bad enough all the bullshit lies Jason had told Nikki, but then that sonofabitch *touched* her? He put his hands on her and actually suggested they get together? What would possess him to tell her all of those lies in the first place? "I guess, after hearing what you just told me, I should be happy that Nikki's even going to dinner with me." I paced, as rage coursed through every single artery in my body.

"That look on your face isn't good. I wasn't going to say anything to you until later tonight or tomorrow, after you talked to her. But I know how your temperament is, you needed to know. I wanted you to be prepared. I wouldn't want you to blow up in front of Nikki. Whatever you do, you need to stay level-headed, and you can't let her know that I said anything to you. I'm pretty sure she's already mad as hell at Jackie, but even madder at me."

I took a deep breath and sighed out slowly. "I'll be fine tonight. Don't worry about that. And I won't say anything, I promise. But it's going to take an army to keep me from beating that fuck within an inch of his life when we get back home."

"I hate to ask this, but I have to know. Is any of what that guy said to Nikki true? Were you having an affair with his wife?"

"Hunter, you know me. Fuck no, it's not true. Not one fucking thing he said was true, except for the fact that she moved in fast and we married fast, but Nikki didn't do anything that she hadn't agreed to. I asked her, and she said yes. Look at me," I said. My eyes were welled with tears, but I didn't care, not now. "I love her. Really, really love her. No, I never cheated on her. I swear."

"I believe you." Hunter shook his head, pushed the chair back, and stood up. "But seriously, you've got some anger issues." He walked over toward the door.

"Hunter," I said. He stopped and turned his head, looking at me over his shoulder. "Thanks, man. Thanks for telling me."

"You're welcome. Enjoy your dinner. You're going to get her back; just be patient. She loves you, even if you are an ass." He laughed, then pulled the door tight as he exited the room.

I flopped on the bed and just stared up at the ceiling. Visions of my fist sinking into Jason's face consumed my thoughts. I knew I couldn't do that without some serious repercussions, but I sure wanted to. I closed my eyes for a few minutes as I thought about how I was going to keep my cool through dinner now that I was aware of what had happened with Nikki at happy hour.

I startled out of my sleep in a panic. I looked at the alarm clock on the bedside table. It was six forty-five. I never meant to fall asleep, let alone sleep so late. I brushed my teeth as fast as I could, put on my shoes, and then rushed around the room making sure I had everything -- keys, wallet, room key, and phone. I darted out of the room and ran down to the elevator.

When I walked down the hallway toward the lobby, I saw her. My palms moistened. I felt warm from head to toe. *Emotion overload.* Anger at what Jason had said and done, sadness that Nikki had to endure that horse shit, fear because I wasn't sure what to expect from her this evening, and love -- pure, undying adoration of my beautiful, strong wife.

She turned toward me when I was a couple of steps from her. "You're late," she said. She had a sadness in her eyes that tugged at each artery connected to my heart.

"I'm sorry. I fell asleep."

Chapter 8

I scratched at my arm while we stood waiting to be seated. The silence between us was uncharacteristic, and it felt weird. Jeff and I normally talked about everything, yet here we were, not talking about anything.

I could feel his eyes on me. Roaming up and down my body. It made me dig my nails into my arm even harder. I wanted to look at him, but I didn't. Instead, I stood there scared to look into the eyes of my own husband. And why? Because I knew he would melt me with his stare, and I couldn't let him do that. My weight shifted from one foot to the other while my eyes remained fixed on the historical poster hanging beside the hostess stand. I don't know why, but I couldn't seem to shake the feeling that he was going to completely devastate me when he told me the truth.

"Carrington," the hostess said.

"Come on, baby." His voice and words came close to unhinging me. I was in such a crazy state of mind. Part of me wanted to run and hide from him. The other part of me wanted to jump into his arms, surrender to him, and let him take me any and every way he wanted. If I gave myself to him right now, though, I'd forfeit my ability to question him. I had to push that thought from my mind. I followed him and the hostess to the table.

"Can I get you two anything to drink?"

I pushed my hair back from my face. "I'd like a glass of Burgundy."

"Make it a bottle of the Chianti, please." Jeff flashed that prize-winning smile at the hostess and made her blush. He turned to me, winked, and smiled. It was just like our first date. Sharing a bottle of wine with dinner. I wondered if he even realized that. I sighed loudly. Probably not.

"Have you eaten here since you've been in town?" Jeff asked. We were sitting in Gallagher's Steakhouse.

"No, I've never been here. How about you?"

"Once, for a business dinner meeting several years ago. Their food is really good, or at least it was back then."

The waitress arrived with our wine. She poured Jeff a small amount in his glass to taste, then, upon his approval, she filled my glass, and then his. It felt like déjà vu.

"Are you ready to order, or do you need a few more minutes?"

"Nikki, are you ready?"

"Uh, um." I sounded like a stammering idiot.

"Want me to order for you?"

I set the menu on the table and raised my hands in the air by my shoulders, palms facing Jeff. "Sure, go for it."

"We'll have two filet mignon, one with a baked potato and green beans for the sides. The other, a side of onion rings."

"Soup or salad?"

"Salads."

"Which dressings would you like?"

"House dressing is fine."

"Perfect. I'll get your order in right away." She turned and walked away.

He knew me like a book. My shoulders relaxed and I leaned back in my seat.

"Are you okay?" he asked.

"I'm fine," I replied. I wasn't sure I was.

We both sipped our wine, with an ominous silence hanging between us.

"Tell me what's going on, darling? One minute we were fine, then the next you're gone. What happened?"

I hated that I appeared emotionally unstable when he spoke to me. There was something about his voice. He sounded more gentle and affectionate than I had ever heard him before. Tears began trickling down my cheeks as my lower lip quivered. I lifted my glass to my lips and took another sip.

With my eyes cast down toward the floor, I began. "I don't know where to start, Jeff. I guess I'll just tell you how my Thursday went after we spoke."

I was interrupted by the waitress bringing our salads. Once she left, I shoveled two bites into my mouth.

I proceeded to tell him about happy hour, and Jason unexpectedly showing up. The waitress brought out our food, which gave me a much-needed break in retelling the events from that evening. When the waitress left, I munched on my onion rings and ate another bite of salad.

I continued to tell Jeff the things Jason had said to me. "He told me Blake was far more beautiful than me, and I was nothing more than a runner-up to her, in your opinion." I watched Jeff's face turn red. He wasn't blushing. I had seen that color change and expression before. He was pissed.

"He followed me out to the car and apologized, then …" I closed my eyes, then lowered my head until my chin touched my chest. I hated even thinking about what that slime ball had done.

"Then what, Nikki?"

I let my hands fall to my side and lifted my head until our eyes met. "Then he forced me --" I swallowed hard. "He, he forced me to kiss him." Jeff blanched. "I took my keys and began hitting and stabbing at him until he finally let me go."

Every drop of blood left Jeff's face. "Before I drove home, I just sat in the car, for nearly a half an hour, crying."

Jeff

I was fucking speechless.

Hearing Hunter tell me the story earlier was completely different than listening to Nikki tell me. I wanted to beat Jason mercilessly. He was a piece of shit to the umpteenth degree. I was close to not giving a shit about possibly having to go to jail for it, either.

I had heard the highlights, but Nikki was providing more detail than Hunter, or apparently, even Jackie knew. I was trying so hard not to scream at the top of my lungs, but I knew I had to remain in control and let her tell me everything. She needed to get it all out.

When she finished talking, her plate of food sat in front of her, mostly untouched. Mine was barely picked at. I had been starving when we walked into the restaurant, but quickly lost my appetite.

The waitress stopped by to ask if everything was okay. She looked concerned. Everything wasn't okay. But it had nothing to do with the food or service.

Now that I had heard everything from her, I had to make sure she heard what I was about to say. It was my turn to convince her exactly what she meant to me. Then it was up to her what she did with our relationship. But God knew, I wanted her more than anything else in the entire world.

I had to bite my tongue and fight to keep my temper in check. I was so enraged after hearing her more in-depth description of that night in the bar. I knew I had to clear up the thought that Blake had gone with me on this last trip immediately. Nikki despised her existence.

"Baby, I told you before, Blake wasn't on that last trip. I don't know why Jason told you that, but her transfer went through, and she wouldn't even have been allowed to go anymore if she wanted to. He should have known that, since she's his wife. I was with Sandy, like I said in my text. I told you that on Thursday when we talked too. I didn't lie to you. Why would I? But for some crazy reason, Jason did. Trust this: I'm not the one trying to ruin us."

"But Jason said she was, and he's her husband. Shouldn't he know where she is?"

She sat and stared at me.

My patience had vanished, and my blood was boiling. "Are you going to take the word of that jitbag over me? Since when are his words more trustworthy than mine, your own husband?"

"I just don't understand why he'd say something like that to me, you know, about Blake being on that trip, if it wasn't true."

"He said a lot to you that wasn't true. Why wouldn't you have just asked me? I had already told you I wasn't with her. The guy proved he was scum with his insinuation that we were together for the sake of a promotion. He continue to show what a jack-off he was with everything else, finishing with saying you were second fiddle to Blake. That's ridiculous. Then he tried to kiss you. Yet you still believed everything he said? Seriously?"

"Jeff, I --"

"I just don't understand why you'd believe him, or leave, Nikki. Why you'd pack up and take the kids, and leave like that." I realized after the words left my mouth that I wasn't helping the situation any, but that didn't stop my fierce tirade.

"I needed to get out of your house. Okay? I needed to clear my head. I didn't want to talk to you, and I didn't want to see you; that's why I left." Her voice was angry and determined.

"You took the coward's way out is what you did. You couldn't even talk to me over the phone. Instead, you ran away and left a cryptic note for me. Like that would be sufficient. What did you think, Nikki? Did you think I'd just sit there and wait for you to come back, or wait to see what you would do next?"

"I was scared, Jeff."

"Of what? Me?"

"I was so afraid of what you'd say. I was scared you'd break my heart into a million pieces." She used the napkin to wipe the tears from her face. "I wasn't thinking straight. I just needed to get out of your damn house before you came home."

"I told you before, don't make assumptions about me, and don't lie to me, because I wouldn't lie to you. You don't trust me, just admit it. You don't even think enough of me to respect me or let me try to explain myself." I threw my napkin on the table.

"That's not true!" she cried.

"I think we both know it is. Your actions proved it. So you came out here to Las Vegas where you don't know anyone. You showed me, didn't you?" I shifted in my seat. "What if someone had attacked you? What if something happened to one of you guys, or one of the kids? What would you do? Do you even think about shit like that?" I ran my fingers through my hair, then leaned across the table toward her. "Do you for one minute know how much that would rip my heart to shreds? Do you care? Jeez, Nikki, you guys are my fucking life."

She lifted her hand to cover her mouth. The tears streamed down her reddened face. The breaths she sucked in through her fingers were labored.

"Damn it!" I was irritated with everything. "I'm sorry I hollered at you. But, babe, you have to know how I feel too. I love you so much. This has to be a two-way street here, not the Nikki Highway. I don't know a whole lot about this, but I thought marriages were *supposed* to work because of open communication. I thought we had that, but right now, we aren't even close. We aren't even anywhere near meeting in the middle. We are the exact opposite of meeting in the middle. I'm giving you everything and what are you giving me, besides a deer-in-headlights look?"

She gasped as if catching her final breath. "I ... I'm sorry."

"Just tell me one thing. I want you to be honest. What's your heart telling you to do? Because mine told me to do whatever I had to do in order to find out where you were. Then I got on that plane and came here to you to so I could make us right."

I sat and watched the tears stream down her face, past her slightly parted lips, and down to the tip of her chin, where the drips slowly fell into her lap. "Are you going to talk to me, baby doll?" Hunter was right. I was a dick. I didn't mean to be, but apparently I fucking sucked at relationships.

She sat and shook her head while she swiped the tears as fast as they fell.

I dug in my pocket and retrieved the crumpled note she had left me.

"Can we at least talk about this note?" I asked. "I think we need to clear the air on a couple of the things you wrote in here."

Her face was flushed a bright shade of pink. "Jeff, I was really upset when I wrote that."

"I understand, but I just think I need to make sure you're crystal clear on a couple things, because I don't want you to question them or me again."

I laid the note out on the table and rubbed my hands over it several times to smooth out the paper as much as I could. "This right here, this is where we should probably start because this had me scratching my head." I pointed at the line that said *I'm glad I was able to help you get what you wanted, but it seems like you won't be needing my services any longer.* "Can you tell me what that means?"

"It never crossed your mind to date me so you'd be considered for a promotion?" she asked.

I inhaled a deep breath and exhaled to the count of five, while I tapped my fingertips on the tabletop. "No, for fuck's sake, I never considered dating you just for a promotion." I pushed my fingers though my hair and sighed. I was surely going to tear hair from my scalp eventually. "Why in the ever loving fuck would I do that?" I had to calm my tone and voice back down. "Jason filled your head with some really crazy shit, and I'm convinced more than ever that he's a complete loon. Honestly, I'm beginning to question you for believing any of what he said."

"I guess he just sounded so convincing."

"You can rest assured, sweetness, I didn't and never, ever, gave that a thought. Jason has a vivid imagination to make that kind of shit up. Connor joked about it in a conversation once before you and I ever even talked on the phone, but it was just that, a joke. He was the one who made the comment, not me. I never gave it a thought. I just replied to him. I'll tell you exactly what he said, and you'll know there was never anything to it."

"Do I need to hear it?"

"Probably not, but because you want to believe asswad and not me, I'll tell you. Then you'll know I'm not hiding anything from you." I leaned back in my seat. "The first Monday you called me and left the message with my assistant, I couldn't call you because I was out of town at a customer site, I told you that. I did talk to Connor later that day with some work-related updates I had to relay to him, and I told him you called. Maybe I was a little excited … maybe." I winked at her. I definitely had been excited when my assistant told me she called, and even more excited when I listened to Nikki's voicemail. "We had talked about you over the weekend after seeing you in the bar on Friday. Anyway, he made the comment that you *could* be Mrs. Carrington, and then I'd get promoted."

"Why would he say something like that?"

"Connor wanted me to get promoted so I could recommend that he be brought over to our team. I told Connor I didn't give a shit about the promotion enough to marry someone just to be considered, period. We never discussed it again. The bottom line is, it was a joke. He wasn't serious."

Nikki sighed.

"And I feel pretty confident that he never said anything to that assclown Jason. Connor and Jason rarely spoke to each other. If anything, Connor's comment to me was overheard and misconstrued. I could ask Connor, but honestly, I'd rather not."

"I'd rather you didn't say anything to him, either."

"You know, I have to tell you, your statement in this note that you were gullible enough to believe I actually loved you really stung, baby. You really have no idea how much I love you, do you?"

Her lips parted, and she began rubbing over the faint scratch marks on her arm; then she leaned back against the chair. She didn't say a word. I watched the tears well in her eyes, and with a slight movement, she shook her head.

"I'm convinced I had been waiting for you all of my life. Before you, I told one woman I loved her."

Nikki's eyes lowered to the ground. I needed her to hear me, and to see me. I leaned my body and stretched my arm across the table, and placed my fingers under her chin, then gently lifted her head so our eyes met. "My mom -- no one else. I've never loved another woman other than my mom, until you. When I told you I loved you, I meant it. And I knew that I'd love you forever because no woman has ever made me feel like you do. Until death do us part, right? If that's not what you want, then, please, say it now."

"I love you so much, Jeff," she muttered. "I think, I didn't realize how much until all of this." Her tears had made their way over her lower lid and fell down her cheeks. "I love you more than I've ever loved anyone."

"You're the only one for me, Nikki. You've always been the only one. I don't know if I can do any more. I don't know if I can give you any more. I don't even know if I can possibly love you any more than I already do. But if I can, I sure as hell will."

I wiped at my eyes. I was on the verge of tears myself. I had never bared myself like that to anyone before, ever.

"Please tell me you won't question my love for you or what you mean to me again. No more thinking there was some big scheme behind moving you in and marrying you? My only plan was to spend the rest of my life with the woman I love, and who says she loves me."

"Yes, we're good. I won't question you again. I promise."

"Good. Next is this statement right here." I pointed to the line about the kids. *The kids and I are no longer going to be a burden to you. If you want to see Alexander, I won't keep him from you.*

"Wait, Jeff. Stop. Let me just say, a lot of this note was written based on the lies Jason told me."

"Then you already know you and the kids aren't a burden? You never have been, and you never will be."

"I get it. I do." She sat and shook her head as she wiped her eyes. "I wanted to believe in us so bad. I was just so scared. Listening to Jason that night, that was my nightmare."

"But that wasn't your reality. That shit Jason spewed, that wasn't real. Our love is real. You and the kids, you're everything to me. Baby, you're my world."

"And you're mine." She reached her hand across the table and rested it on top of mine. What I wouldn't have given to feel her body pressed tight against me.

"It's getting late. I guess you need to get back to the kids. But let's meet for breakfast, and bring the kids with you."

Her eyes were focused on the floor while she bit her lower lip. She was hesitating. "Okay, I'll meet you."

We stepped into the elevator and rode up to her floor. Even though we had talked, I got the feeling something was still troubling her. I wanted so badly to pull her into my arms and kiss away all of her worry and uncertainty about us. It was killing me not to touch her.

"I'll see you at nine in the lobby. Is that plenty of time to get the kids ready?"

"Yeah."

Chapter 9

By the time we left the restaurant, I felt like I had run a full marathon. My body and mind were exhausted. I needed to get back to my room, where I could just think about everything.

Jason had been so matter-of-fact when he told me the 'truths' at the bar. But when I listened to Jeff, and looked into his eyes, I knew he wasn't lying to me.

I just didn't understand why Jason would lie. What did he have to gain from making all of that stuff up? I think that was the question that was really eating at me.

But Jason hadn't made up everything he said. Some things were still true. Jeff *did* move me in fast, he did seem like he was rushing our relationship, and he did propose in front of *his* coworkers and manager. But I had agreed to all of that.

And Jeff had also been seeing Blake.

But if Jeff really wanted to get rid of me like Jason had said, why did he come after me? Why would he fly all the way to Las Vegas? He could have just let me go. And I knew he loved Alexander and Abby. They didn't seem to be burdens to him at all. I couldn't believe I fell for Jason's lies. I felt like such a complete moron.

The picnic situation was still a mystery. I know what Jeff said, and I know what Jason said. I also knew my eyes hadn't deceived me when I looked in that bedroom and saw Blake's hands on Jeff as they talked. Thinking back to that day wasn't good. I had to brush off the sinking feeling that started to consume me all over again. I may never know the true story about that situation. But until someone proved otherwise, I had to believe Jeff.

I swiped my room key card through the slot and crept into the room, hoping not to wake anyone, but the light was on. I knew someone was up.

"How was your date?" Jessica asked.

"I'd hardly call it a date, but it went fine."

"Everything worked out?"

"No, not completely. We're going to meet for breakfast, and I'll be taking the kids."

"That's good. That's a step in the right direction. How did the talk go tonight?"

"It went pretty good, I guess. I'm still a little confused, though. He told me Jason was lying."

"That's what you were hoping he'd say, right?"

"Yeah, I was, but …" I drifted off as my thoughts began rehashing the questions still floating around in my head.

"I don't mean to question you, but aren't you being a little hard on him? He has to get some credit for flying all the way here to see you. And he told you what you had hoped he'd say."

"I know. I think I just need to get some sleep. I just need some time to let this all sink in."

"Just so you know, tomorrow morning, I'm going to meet up with Ben. He asked me earlier, and now that I know you'll have the kids, I'll take him up on it."

"That's fine. Stay out of trouble." I winked at her. "I'll text with you and let you know how things are going. But you have fun."

"I plan to. Good night."

"Good night, Jessica."

Chapter 10

It took every single bit of energy to roll over and turn off that blaring alarm. I had slept terribly. Maybe it was the nap before dinner, or the uneasy feeling I got from Nikki as we parted ways last night. Whatever it was, I wished I could sleep for another couple of hours now.

After getting ready, I made my way down to the lobby and saw my beauty standing with Alexander in her arms, his diaper bag hanging from one shoulder, and her purse on the other. Abby stood nearby, clutching a toy.

"Good morning." I walked up and gave Alexander a kiss on his chubby cheek. He gave me a big smile in return and cooed. Then I bent down to give Abby a big hug. I desperately wanted to kiss Nikki's perfect lips. I needed to feel her in my arms again, soon.

"Good morning," Nikki said. "Where are we going?"

"Are you up for a walk to MGM Grand? They have an awesome brunch buffet."

"But it's still breakfast time." I couldn't help but notice she seemed more at ease than the night before.

"They stopped serving breakfast at nine, so it's officially brunch time."

"All right, then I guess we're having brunch."

"Yay, brunch." Abby danced around while Nikki and I chuckled.

I reached over and took Alexander from her. She didn't need to carry him. The walk wasn't that far, but my little guy could get heavy pretty quick, and he wiggled a lot. Plus, I just wanted to hold my son. She held Abby's hand, and we made our way to the path.

We reached the buffet and were seated immediately, then given the go-ahead to serve ourselves. Abby bounced around in the line. She was bubbling over with excitement at the variety of foods. She wanted all of the pastries and sweets to be put on her plate. Nikki persuaded her to get a small piece of waffle because it was just like cake, then she could have something sweet. Abby's face lit up with a huge smile as she nodded her head enthusiastically in agreement.

We kept the conversation light while we ate. I could tell that Nikki had something on her mind, but discussing any of this in front of Abby wasn't going to happen.

"Abby," I said. Her head popped up like a little ground squirrel. "Would you like to go see some pretty flowers today, or go to the Aquarium to see some really big fish?"

She sat in deep thought, her little fist resting under her chin, and her eyes wandering around the room. She dropped her hand to the table and propelled her tiny body up straight. "Fish!" she screamed.

Nikki and I laughed. Our eyes met, and, for that brief moment, her guard had been dropped.

"Where's an aquarium?" she asked.

"There are two. The small one is down on the far end of the strip, and the other is right on the other side of the Luxor Hotel, inside the Mandalay Bay. Do you have a preference?"

"The larger one."

"Perfect."

Nikki

Jeff was too perfect. His attentiveness was making me think thoughts I shouldn't be thinking right now. I had to ask him my questions while Abby was glued to the aquarium wall, mesmerized, and distracted, by the fish. I just hoped it didn't put a damper on the day.

"Why was I the one you decided to be with?"

"What?" Jeff looked down at me, and I turned my gaze away from him. I couldn't look at him. I couldn't let our eyes meet or I would have disintegrated. "Well, that's not an easy question to answer. I guess it's the old saying, you love who you love."

"You weren't even interested in me. I practically chased you down." I picked the loose hair off of my shirt and watched it drop to the ground.

"Listen to yourself. You sound crazy. The only reason I hesitated was because I had just recently become single. I didn't know if I wanted to jump right back into dating or a relationship. But hear me, I definitely noticed you in the restaurant."

"You were late and unapologetic the first time you meet me. And you seemed so standoffish. You didn't act like you were interested at all."

"I can't believe you just said that to me. Do you really think that? If I wasn't interested back then, we wouldn't be standing here right now. We wouldn't have even met that first time."

Alexander began his squirming routine, and began to cry.

"Give him to me," I said. I reached my arms out to take him from Jeff.

"I can handle his fussiness."

"I'm still breastfeeding him, and he's hungry. Give him to me, please." My impatience had to have been showing on my face. "I'll give him back after he eats."

"I thought you were stopping this past week since you went back to work?"

"I was trying, but he couldn't keep the formula down. I had planned to tell you on Friday. So, here we are."

"But the bottles? I thought they were all formula?"

"No, not all of them. I was using a pump, too, while I tried the formula out, just in case. I've kept using it. I just forgot to bring it with me."

"Well, I guess you have to do what's best for our son, right?"

"Exactly."

We found a bench sitting back in a darker section of the aquarium. Once I was seated and comfortable, I held my son to my breast. Abby came running over.

"Is baby hungry, Mommy?"

"Yes, he is. Are you going to hold his hand?"

"Yep." Abby held one of Alexander's hands in hers, while his other hand was tightly grasping my shirt. Abby liked holding Alexander's hand while I fed him. It was something she started doing after Jeff went back to work. I draped a cloth over myself to keep from being exposed to everyone else in the room.

My mind flashed back to the nights at home while Jeff was on leave from work. We'd sit together in the lounge chair in our room, I'd snuggle between his legs with his arms wrapped around me while I fed Alexander. He often times had rubbed my back with one hand and rubbed Alexander's head with the other. I missed those times. I missed being held in his arms. And I missed that bond we had formed together in those weeks.

When Alexander was done, I stood up and handed Jeff a cloth. "Lay that across your shoulder, and you can burp him."

He had watched me as I performed this post-feeding ritual many times. I was sure he was capable of this, and was ready to let him give it a try. He had balked in the past because he thought Alexander was too small and he said he felt like he was hitting him too hard on his back. Instead he let me take care of it.

Once he was successful in his first burping attempt, Jeff raised Alexander above his head. "That's my big boy." They both smiled, and Jeff laughed. They celebrated like they had won a first-place trophy.

I laughed at them. "You two are ridiculous! Is this what I have to look forward to? A celebration of burps?"

Alexander's smile was infectious, and hearing Jeff giggle had me giddy inside. I couldn't stop laughing. Even Abby was laughing.

"Maybe it is," Jeff said.

Chapter 11

Her words gave me hope.

"Tell me what you want, sweetheart." I placed my fingers under her chin and held her so our eyes were fixed on each other. "Jason told you a bunch of crazy shit. I'm telling you he's a freaking nut job. So I need you to tell me, where do we go from here?"

"We may not be perfect, but I don't want to give up. I just need to know, since we've been married, has there ever been anything between you and Blake that wasn't work related?"

"No, never." I was agitated that she asked me that question. It was as if she didn't know me at all. And she was really having a hard time letting go of her unjustified jealousy of Blake. "The woman means absolutely nothing to me. Nothing. Period."

The relationship talk between us stopped at that moment. Abby and Alexander were both getting restless as we made it through the Shark Reef. I knew it was probably time for Nikki and me to leave. We both turned our focus to the kids, and getting them back to the room.

While on our walk back to the hotel, my phone rang.

I shifted Alexander from one arm to the other, then pulled my phone out of my pocket. It was Hunter. "Hey."

"What's going on? How's things going with Nikki?"

"We're on our way back to the hotel now. The kids were getting fidgety."

"Where were you guys?"

"After brunch, we went to the Aquarium in Mandalay Bay."

"I had no idea there was an Aquarium there. We'll come by Nikki's room and meet up with you guys."

"Okay, later," I said, then pressed end to disconnect.

"That was Hunter. He and Jackie are going to come by your room."

"Oh, good. I need to talk to her anyway." The look on her face led me to believe Jackie had some explaining to do. And if she had to explain, that meant Hunter would have to explain. I'd have to make sure I was around because I couldn't just leave them both to face Nikki's questioning alone. I had to make sure I was there to beg for forgiveness for asking Hunter to help me. But I sure as hell wasn't going to apologize for being in Las Vegas to win her back.

Jessica wasn't in the room when we returned. Abby ran to the remote and turned on the television, then climbed on the bed.

"Where's Jessica?" I asked.

"She met some guy down by the pool a few days ago. They've been texting non-stop. She told me last night she was going to meet up with him today."

"Has she gone out with him before now?"

"Yeah, she went out to dinner with him not long after she met him."

We were interrupted by the knock on the door. Nikki went and opened it to let Jackie and Hunter in.

"Oh, look who it is," Nikki said. She closed the door behind them.

"Hey, guys," Jackie said. She seemed a little more uncertain about what to say than I had ever seen her. "I guess I owe you an apology, Nikki. And I probably owe you one too, Jeff."

"Don't sweat it, Jackie. We're cool." I couldn't help but wonder what Hunter said to her to get her to admit she should apologize to me.

"We'll talk," Nikki said. Her eyes said everything there was to say. If it was possible to cut someone with a gaze, Jackie would have been sliced all the way to the bone. I thought Nikki was being too hard on her, but I wasn't sure what they had discussed before our arrival.

Nikki turned her glare toward Hunter. "And you ..."

I had to stop her. She needed to remember these were our friends. They had both been put in a bad situation. It wasn't their fault. They should never have had to choose who they were going to be loyal to.

"Nikki, it's all my fault," I said. "If I hadn't begged Hunter to help me to find you, he never would have put pressure on Jackie to tell him where you guys were. Baby, I had to see you. I had to come talk to you. It's all my fault. I'm not sorry for one second that I'm here, but please, don't take it out on them."

Her shoulders relaxed, and her eyes filled with tears. Jackie walked over and gave her best friend a hug, while whispering how sorry she was in Nikki's ear.

"Let us make it up to you, Nikki," Jackie said.

Nikki

I really wasn't mad at Jackie anymore. Or Hunter. I really liked them both a lot and didn't want to jeopardize our friendship.

Instead, I was curious what was going on with them. I glanced back and forth between the two of them. I hadn't seen or heard from Jackie since Hunter and Jeff had shown up. Before they got here, she crashed in our room one night. Her room was right next door to mine.

"What do you have in mind?" I asked Jackie.

"We can watch the kids for you guys. Tonight, or sometime when we get back home," she said.

"Maybe when we get back home. What I want to know right now is what's going on between you two?" I waved my finger back and forth, pointing at Jackie, then over at Hunter. "Are you two a couple?"

Jackie and Hunter looked at each other and laughed. I felt silly for insinuating they were dating. They were laughing at me. I just couldn't understand why Jackie would tell Hunter where we were, or why she conveniently disappeared for more than an entire day.

Chapter 12

 Nikki

"Wait a minute. You two *are* a couple?" I asked. There was something about the exchange of glances between them. I turned and saw the smirk on Jeff's face. "Did you know?"

Jeff smiled at me. "Yes, but I just found out not too long ago."

"Like, how long ago?"

"Sometime after I went back to work," he said. He turned and shook his head at Hunter. "You guys did a really good job keeping it a secret."

"Wait," I said. It took everything inside me to keep myself from jumping around to get their attention. I couldn't believe my best friend had been hiding this from me. "Why wouldn't you say anything to me? You could have told me, right?" I asked Jackie.

"I could have, you're right, Nikki. But I didn't because I wanted to make sure what we had going on was real. I wanted to make sure he was the one before I said anything. I didn't want the wedding wheels in your head to begin spinning, just for you to find out a couple months later that we aren't a couple anymore."

"So when did you guys start seeing each other? How did I miss this?"

"We talked during the rehearsal dinner," Hunter said. "Then afterward, we went to a movie, and talked some more. The chemistry between us was perfect. So we exchanged phone numbers, and after talking and texting a lot, we decided to go out again a couple days later."

"And Jackie's nickname is Chipmunk," Jeff said, shaking his head. He scrunched his mouth and nose as if he tasted something bitter.

"Aw, that's so cute," I replied.

"Yeah." Jeff snickered for a couple seconds, then went into a deep belly laugh. He gave Hunter a shove, knocking him slightly off balance, which, in turn, caused Hunter to laugh.

 *Jeff*

"Chipmunk, how about you and Jackrabbit here join us for dinner tonight?" I couldn't stop laughing at her freaking nickname. Alexander smiled too. But he grinned every time anyone else did.

"What about the kids?" Jackie asked.

"They are part of the *us* going to dinner. We aren't leaving them. They need to eat too."

They exchanged those googly-eyed glances, raising their eyebrows at each other without saying a word, as if they were speaking in code. With a final shrug of his shoulders, Hunter finally replied. "Yeah, sure, we'll go. It'll be fun."

"We're going to dinner, not an amusement park." I laughed at him. "Seven o'clock in the lobby. Is pizza good, or would you all rather go to the Burger Bar?"

Abby sat up and chanted, "Pizza, pizza, pizza."

"There's three votes for pizza. Anyone else?" Nikki asked.

Everyone couldn't agree on pizza, so we decided going to America's was best. They had everything. I was so happy this day was working out as I had hoped. I really wanted to just grab something quick to eat, hang out with our friends for a couple of hours, then my plan was to get Nikki and the kids in my room for the night.

"Baby, text Jessica and let her know if she wants to stop by, she's welcome to. And tell her she doesn't need to worry about watching the kids tonight."

****

It felt surreal sitting at the table with everyone. An impromptu trip that had the footprint of a personal catastrophe for not just Nikki and me, but also for Hunter and Jackie, had been triumphant for all. Jessica and her friend, Bill, or Bob, or Bart, or whatever his name was, joined us.

The kids were happy. Abby had a huge slice of pizza on her plate that she'd never be able to eat, but it didn't matter. The smile on her adorable face was priceless. Alexander was prematurely tasting pizza crust for the first time. That wasn't something we'd necessarily share with his pediatrician at his next appointment, though. Hunter and Jackie were all smiles and kissy-faced now that their secret was out in the open.

Everyone was having a good time. The table was abuzz with conversations about nearly everything imaginable. Best of all, I had my girl back by my side. There was still some unresolved business, but we could work on that later.

This seemed like the perfect time to tell Nikki my good news that I'd had to put on the back burner. It had been killing me not to tell her before now because I knew this was something she had been waiting to hear.

"Baby, I have some fantastic news," I said. "I've been dying to tell you since I found out on Friday."

"Shh, everyone," Nikki said. She got everyone to quiet down. "Jeff has something to say. Go ahead, babe, tell us." She leaned toward me with a wide smile on her face.

"Well, baby doll, how would you feel about me being at home with you every night?"

She gulped in a huge breath. "Jeff, no! Really?"

"Really. I was told just before I flew home. That was my final trip for quite a while."

"That's awesome, man," Hunter said. Jackie smiled and gave me a thumbs-up.

"I'll have to travel maybe two or three times a year, but the rest of the time, I'll be home with you and the kids." I tapped my hand on top of her intertwined fingers.

"That's the best news ever, baby." Nikki's eyes watered and she smiled at me. She reached over and clasped her arms around my neck, then pulled me toward her until my lips were on hers.

Chapter 13

 Jeff

When dinner ended, Jessica and her friend left to continue exploring the town. The rest of us climbed into the elevator. Abby was rubbing her eyes and Alexander had his head on my shoulder, fast asleep. Nikki stood just inches in front of me.

"Stay with me tonight," I whispered in Nikki's ear. My fingers twirled the ends of her flowing blonde strands. She leaned her head back against my chest and nodded yes. My head dipped as I inhaled her scent deep into my soul.

We said good night to Hunter and Jackie, then went into my room. I made a phone call to the front desk to get a crib brought up. Abby could sleep on the pullout sofa. I was sure she'd like that since there was a television in there.

After housekeeping left, Alexander was moved from my bed to the crib, which had been set up near the sofa. We had the bed made for Abby and the television on already. Judging by the look in her eyes, she wasn't going to be awake for much more than a few minutes.

After we both kissed Abby goodnight, we went back into the bedroom, but left the door ajar just enough to hear if either of them cried out.

I watched as Nikki situated Alexander's things across the desk in case we had to get up in the night. God, she was beautiful. I thought back to the last time I had made love to her. Back before she gave birth to Alexander. She was so stunning then, too, as she waddled around with my baby inside of her.

I pulled off my T-shirt and tossed it on the back of the chair.

"I need a shirt, Jeff. If I have to get up in the middle of the night, I prefer not to walk naked in front of the kids."

My cock perked up at her words. I wanted to see and feel her naked form. I retrieved a shirt for her. "Here."

"What's wrong?" She tilted her head slightly to the side.

"Nothing's wrong, baby. I'm just finding it so hard to keep my hands off of you." I raised my hand up to rub down her silky hair. That minute of a touch sent chills through me.

"Who said you had to," she whispered. "I'm yours." Her eyes closed, and she leaned her head into my hand that was still in her hair.

"Let's make that official again." I reached into my pocket and pulled out her rings. I had been carrying them with me all day, hoping for this moment. She gasped when she saw what I had, and held her trembling hand out for me.

"With these rings, baby." I slid them on her finger, where they belonged. "I think you know the rest."

"Jeff, I need you to touch me. I need to feel your arms wrapped around me."

I grabbed a handful of her hair at her nape, pulled her in tight, and lowered my mouth onto hers. "You're my world, baby doll. You're the only one for me." My lips found hers again. She melted against me as tears streamed down her face.

I pulled back from her. "Baby, don't cry."

"I feel so stupid, though." Nikki shook her head. "I should have talked to you. I was trying to shield my heart. I'm so sorry for not talking to you first, Jeff."

"We're talking now. I don't want you to feel funny. I didn't search for you to make you feel bad. I wanted you to know I love you more than anything." I kissed her forehead. "Promise me one thing, doll."

"Anything, just name it."

"Please, never leave me again, baby."

"Never," she whispered. I lowered my mouth onto hers. She was mine.

❧ Nikki ❧

I felt like I was floating on air. His kiss, his touch, the spicy musk smell of his cologne intermingled with his own unique scent -- it was all overloading my senses.

His arms wrapped around me tight, holding me in place against his firm, muscled chest. He consumed me like he had been starving, and I was his sustenance.

His hands clambered up and down my yearning body. He set my body alight each time he touched a new spot.

My hands grasped at him. I needed him. I could feel a fire burning down there, and my essence was pooling between my thighs. I needed him to quench this unbelievable thirst deep inside my core. I had to have him.

He nudged me backwards until I felt the back of my legs touch the edge of the bed. Our lips never parted. Holding me by my head, his hands wrapped in my hair, he leaned me back. He eased me down onto the bed. I fucking loved when he pulled my hair. It was so animalistic, so beastlike -- so him.

He laid on the bed next to me, then skimmed his lips across mine. "Damn, Nikki." His fingers stayed tangled in my hair while he refamiliarized himself with my curves using the other hand. "Fuck, baby." His mouth descended on mine, and I met his tongue with my own. I drank in his taste.

I pulled him toward me, while turning my body to meet his. We lay face-to-face, as my hands caressed his stubbled cheeks and roamed freely over his shirtless, chiseled torso. I broke our hold on each other for a brief moment; just long enough to tell him something I knew he needed to hear. "I love you, babe."

The hand that was wrapped in my hair pulled me to him as he owned my mouth, while his other hand slid between my skin and the fabric of my shorts. I could feel the wetness. I wanted to give everything to him. I wanted everything from him.

"Slide up on the bed and take those shorts off." I did as I was instructed. He stared at me as I lay propped up on my elbows, in place like he wanted. My body shivered under his gaze.

Chapter 14

Just watching this delicate creature on the bed, shivering in anticipation of my next move, nearly made me come apart.

I climbed up on the bed, up her silky-smooth body, and on to her perfect lips. My tongue lashed at hers, licking the taste of her into my mouth. She eagerly parted her lips for me, to let my tongue search the depths of her.

I let my tongue glide down her perfect neck, down between her breasts, down her stretch-marked belly. "Lay back all the way, baby." Once she was flat on the bed, I continued my pursuit of my rainbow. My tongue resumed right where I had left off, beginning just below her belly button. I stopped at her C-section scar and showered her with kisses along that jagged line from the left side all the way to the right. The most precious gift she could have ever given me was responsible for that mark. And I'd love her every day for it. I'd worship that scar until the day I died.

I resumed my descent, gliding down, down, down over her mound and into her heat. Her smell and taste made me ravenous. My fingers eased her lips apart, while my tongue laved at her nectar. My triangular jewel.

It had been so long since I'd touched her down there. I felt as giddy as a kid in a candy shop to be able to lick and suck her clit. "Mmm, Jeff." To hear her moans. To run my tongue along her inner haven.

Her hands weaved in my hair, pulling me gently tighter to her. My tongue extended and delved deep in her core, but was quickly replaced by my finger. "Damn, baby." Her wetness increased as the seconds ticked by. As much as I couldn't wait to sink my cock in her, I wanted to make sure she was wound tight, then unfurled into the most intense orgasm before I let her silky heat sheath me.

As I worked my finger in and out of her, my lips captured her clit and I sucked my pearl. I added a second finger to her hole and her moans grew louder.

"You better keep it down or you'll wake up the kids," I warned. She muffled her mewls. My fingers continued to pump inside her. I moved my thumb up to caress over her clit.

"Damn, baby, I need to feel you inside of me."

"Soon, doll."

I continued to work her. She raised her hips to meet the thrusting of my fingers. I held her down on the bed, and used my tongue to massage her clit until she stifled a scream. Her walls clenched tighter than I remembered around my fingers, pulling them deeper inside her canal. Her breaths were ragged and labored. She sounded more like a wild animal panting as she dragged air in and out of her lungs.

I stood and pulled my shorts and underwear down over my hips, freeing my cock. Slowly, I crawled back onto the bed, finding my place between her smooth thighs. This was home, this was my Heaven. I lowered my head to lap her juices from her, then returned to my kneeling position, where I prepared to seat myself balls deep in her.

I eased inside her, inch by inch. I pressed deeper until I felt our moist skin meet.

⚒ Nikki ⚒

The ache deep inside my walls could only be remedied by one thing. I needed him inside me. I squirmed under the handiwork of his skilled fingers, but my core quivered on the inside in anticipation of him filling me. He was driving me completely mad.

As he stood to remove his shorts, my tongue caressed over my bottom lip before my teeth bit down gently. My hips rolled forward; I was eager and excited to feel him. He was gorgeous, and he was mine. I needed him so bad.

His glorious body climbed back up on the bed, making his way up to me, positioning himself between my open legs. He licked between my flesh before he entered me. After three long months of his absence, it felt like I was virginal all over again as he pressed deeper, stretching my walls, making room for himself inside me. And I welcomed every single millimeter of his manhood.

A low moan escaped my lips as I felt our skin meet. The fullness was incredible. He lowered his head and covered my mouth with his, letting me taste myself on him. Our tongues collided while he took his time easing in and out of me, making love to me. My arms snaked around his neck as I pulled him down on me. I just wanted to hold Jeff and never let him go. I wanted us to stay just like this, feeding off each other until we were sated and could no longer move.

His hands slid down my sides and reached under my ass, pulling me up to him, tighter around him. "Fuck, baby," he moaned. "You feel so damn good."

Jeff's thrusts were getting harder, and the hotel bed was squeaking and creaking under our weight. I didn't want him to stop, but the thought of waking the kids was something I wanted even less. I squeezed my legs tight around his waist and put my hand firmly on his hip to stop him from pummeling me any further.

"Is everything okay, Nikki? Was I hurting you?" he asked.

"No, you weren't hurting me. Jeez, babe, you feel so good. But the bed is making way too much noise."

"Shit, baby, I don't want to stop."

"I don't want you to," I whispered. "But I don't want the kids to wake up, either."

"You get on top; maybe that will help." Jeff rolled onto his back, and I straddled him. He lifted my hips up, and I positioned him at my opening, then he slowly loosened his grip and I slid down his length, taking him all in. He grabbed a handful of my hair, causing me to whimper as he pulled me down, our chests pressed tight together, and our mouths on each other. His taste, mixed with my essence made me want to scream.

"I love you, baby," Jeff said, his lips skimming mine. I noticed a tear sliding down his temple.

"I love you, too," I managed. My tears fell on his face before I lowered myself on him, wrapping my arms behind him, around his neck. "God, I fucking love you so much." My tears dripped into his hair.

His hands clasped my ass-cheeks, and his thrusts were hard. I could feel him getting close. I was so weak, I laid on him and kissed his neck, his ear, then snaked my tongue up the side of his face to his mouth. "Forever, baby, me and you."

"Ahh, damn! Baby, fuck." Jeff bit down gently on my shoulder as he tried to muffle his voice.

I threw my head back as my core tightened around him, milking him. "Mmm," I moaned. I felt his hot seed filling me as my core gripped his cock, and fireworks shot off behind my eyelids.

He pulled me back down into him, crushing my mouth on top of his. We lay holding each other, kissing each other, loving each other. This was where I belonged. I had second and triple guessed us for far too long.

I laid my head on Jeff's shoulder with his arms wrapped around me tight. Slowly, his grip loosened, then I heard him begin to snore. I was able to wiggle out of his grasp and get to the bathroom, where I wet a washcloth and came back in to clean him up. My hand touched his thigh, and he jumped.

"It's okay, baby, just relax," I whispered. I inhaled the scent of our love before I took the warm cloth and wiped him gently, making sure to get as much of our co-mingled juices cleaned off as I could. I returned to the bathroom to rinse the cloth and cleaned myself up as well. I almost hated to wipe him away.

Before I got back in the bed, I slipped on the T-shirt Jeff had given me, then walked out to the living room to check on Abby and Alexander. Both were sleeping soundly.

I tiptoed back into the room and climbed in bed. Jeff pulled me in tight against his body, spooning his strong, muscled physique around me as his arm draped over my waist.

"Good night, baby doll." Jeff's breath on my neck followed by the soft kisses sent shivers down my spine before I relaxed back into him.

I interlaced my fingers in his and lifted his hand to my mouth, kissing it gently. "Good night."

Chapter 15

We were woke up in the morning to the sound of the crib being kicked and Abby pulling at Nikki's toes.

"Mommy, Mommy, Mommy," she said.

"What do you need, Abby?" I asked.

"I need Mommy." Abby's voice was laced with concern.

I nudged Nikki, but she had already began to wake. "What's wrong, baby?"

"Mommy, the baby is mad." No sooner had the words come out of her mouth, Alexander started to scream at the top of his lungs. I jumped up, pulling the top blanket with me. I left the sheet for Nikki. She had the oversized T-shirt on, but no underwear.

I ducked into the bathroom and quickly put on my underwear and shorts, washed my face and hands, then went into the living room area to get my son.

"Hey, Alexander." I lifted him up and held him close to my face. His little fingers grabbed at me, trying to get a grip. His frown was replaced with a big smile. "How's my boy? Huh?"

Abby came running into the room with us. "Pick me up." Her arms were outstretched toward me, and she had a huge smile on her face. Nikki walked in and took Alexander from me. With free hands, I bent and scooped Abby up under her arms and, in one non-stop motion, raised her up so her cute little face was over my head. She giggled uncontrollably. We did that several times; it was like a workout.

"Down. I need to potty," Abby screeched.

I set her feet on the ground, and she took off running to the bathroom.

"I'm going to get started packing, babe." I leaned down and kissed Nikki's head while she fed Alexander.

After I finished packing, and Alexander was fed and changed, I got checked out of my room, and we made our way to Nikki's room. Nikki sent a text to Jessica to let her know we were on our way.

Our flight didn't leave until later in the afternoon. We took our luggage to the front desk, got something to eat, then we all went to sit out by the pool while we waited for Jackie and Hunter to come join us.

 *Nikki*

A million thoughts were racing through my mind. Tops on the list was the replay of last night with Jeff. I situated the rings on my finger. What an amazing way to end a really awesome day. Brunch, then the Aquarium, which was so much nicer than I had expected. But last night was the best, by far. Being in his arms again, having him make love to me.

My sex clenched at the memory, and I inhaled deeply. He reached his hand over, clasping mine in his. We looked at each other and smiled. Perfect.

We sat by the pool for about an hour, then, after Hunter and Jackie made their way down to meet up with us, we decided to walk around the shops for an hour or so.

We gathered all of our luggage, loaded it and everyone into the cars, and then made our way to the car rental return.

By the time we got to the airport, another thought had made its way to the forefront of my mind -- the thought of having to face my boss, Jack, that asshole Jason's brother. I think he had been relieved when I called and told him I'd be taking a few days off. I wasn't looking forward to a conversation with him about that night at all, but I knew it was inevitable. I couldn't see any way around it. I wish there was.

"Are you okay, baby? You look like something's bothering you," Jeff said.

"Oh, no, I'm okay."

"Maybe we'll talk later, after we get home, yeah?"

"Yeah," I said. My voice was low as my mind drifted back to Jack.

My eyes followed Abby as she made her way between Jessica, Jackie, and Hunter. What I wouldn't give to be young and carefree again. She had it made. Not a worry in the world.

Jeff got us checked in and our luggage checked. He still had his first-class ticket and Hunter had his for the return flight. Jackie, Jessica, the kids, and I were back in coach, which was fine with me. It was quite ironic that we just so happened to all be on the same flight home.

We made it through the security line without any delays. Even Jeff made it past the checkpoint this time without being stopped.

"I'm going to stop in this little shop," I said.

Everyone stopped and waited while Abby and I went in to get water, soda pops, and juice for us all to have on the plane. We walked down to our gate and sat across the aisle from where we needed to be, since there were plenty of available seats. It also gave Abby a little more room to move around without interrupting other people. Alexander had fallen asleep in Jeff's arms and was being held snug against his chest.

"I think I'm going to give Jackie my seat, and I'll sit back with you and the kids," Jeff whispered in my ear.

"You don't have to. You have more leg room up there."

"I'd rather be with you." He tilted his head to the side and lowered his mouth onto mine.

"I'd rather you be with me too."

Jeff turned his focus to Jackie and Hunter. I couldn't help but laugh at the two of them. They were huddled together, whispering, kissing, and staring into each other's eyes. They made such a cute couple. It still boggled my mind that they had kept their relationship hidden from me for so long. Had I been so absorbed in my own life that I never realized what was going on right under my own nose?

"Jackie," Jeff said.

She startled at hearing her name. "Yes?" she answered.

"Here, you sit up with Hunter." He held out his boarding pass for her to take. "Give me your boarding pass."

"Thanks, but you don't have to do that, Jeff."

"I know I don't *have* to. I want to. I'd rather sit with Nikki, and I'm sure Hunter would rather you sit by him, instead of being forced to sit next to me again."

"Where do I get to sit?" Abby asked. Her little hands were drumming Jeff's leg and the empty seat next to him.

"You have to sit by me," Jeff said.

"Yay." She clapped and hopped around. I knew she would go between where we sat and the seat beside Jessica, if it was empty.

Chapter 16

By the time we landed in Tampa, I think we were all so happy to be back home. I was even happier still that I wouldn't have to fly again for quite some time.

We got our luggage, and made it out to the car. It was a puzzle trying to figure out how to get everything in the cars, and everybody. Fortunately, Hunter and Jackie offered to take Jessica back to our house.

I drove us in Nikki's car. I was glad I drove and that it was so quiet. Her car made a funny noise and had a rattle coming from the rear. I'd have to make sure it went into the shop.

The drive was quiet. I knew Nikki's thoughts had been on getting back to work, and her boss. I never told her, but so many times I wished she would just quit. Now, after this bullshit with Jason, knowing that asshat was her boss's brother, I really wanted to tell her to just give her notice and leave that place. But I wasn't going to say anything. She'd have to decide how to handle this. But if that was her choice, she'd get no argument from me.

We made it home in record time. I helped Nikki get the kids in the house. Both were fast asleep. Nikki took Abby in to the bathroom while I changed Alexander's diaper, then laid him in his crib. He never woke, but I knew he'd be up early in the morning. I heard Jessica come in and lock the door.

As soon as I walked into our bedroom, Nikki stepped out of the bathroom wearing an oversized T-shirt. "Jeff, you really don't have to go out of town anymore?"

"Nope, I'll be in the local office starting tomorrow. I have a meeting at ten o'clock, so as long as I'm in before the meeting starts, I'm good."

She ran toward me and wrapped her arms around my neck, and pulled me down onto her minty-fresh mouth.

"You better get some sleep. I think you have a long day ahead of you tomorrow," I said.

"Ugh, don't remind me." She lolled her head back and rolled her eyes.

I had a burning question that I needed to ask her, but it would have to wait until the next night. I wasn't going to keep her up. Instead, we climbed in bed and I pulled her body in close to mine, then wrapped my arms around her. "Good night, doll." I kissed her on the neck and snuggled my head close to hers.

"Good night."

****

We woke the next morning to the earsplitting sound of the alarm. No sooner had Nikki gotten out of the bed, Alexander began to fuss.

"Go take your shower. I'll get him." I dragged myself out of the bed, slipped on my pajama pants, and was asking myself how the hell Nikki was able to get ready for work and take care of the kids each morning, and still get to work on time. By the time I reached Alexander, I could hear Jessica's alarm going off.

"Good morning, baby boy," I called to Alexander. He had a grip on one of the rails.

He cooed at me. I pretended to understand what he was trying to say, and just smiled. Hell, I didn't understand him at all. Nikki probably did, though. If she were here, she could have interpreted for me.

I got him changed just as Jessica shuffled into the bedroom. Her slippers scraped against the carpet. That sound really irritated me. "Good morning, Jessica."

"Good morning." She kept shuffling over to Abby's bed and gave her a little shake. "Abby, time to get up." Her voice was soft. Abby rolled over toward her with a big grin on her face. She was the happiest kid upon waking.

Alexander and I made our way down to the kitchen. "Should we make coffee for Mommy?" I asked him.

He giggled. He was probably quite amused at my ridiculous-sounding voice. I didn't know how to talk to a baby. I had heard Nikki and was following her lead. The way she talked to Alexander sounded so natural. She was meant to be a mom. I don't believe being a parent was what I was supposed to do, but I was one, and I was trying to learn how to be a good one.

I set Alexander in his bouncy seat, while I got the coffee started. I wasn't sure how much time Nikki would have, but I decided to make her an egg sandwich. She could either eat it at home if she had time, or take it with her.

It didn't take long for Jessica and Abby to make their way down to the kitchen. Jessica stood and stared at me while I put the eggs on the toast. She shook her head and plugged in the waffle maker, then retrieved the box of waffle mix from the cupboard. After stirring in an egg, some olive oil, and a little milk, she poured the mix into the waffle maker and closed the lid. Abby sat nearby watching the waffle maker. *That didn't look too hard. I could do that*, I thought.

"Are you eating the sandwich?" Jessica asked. I could tell by the sound of her voice she was a little annoyed. I had no idea why.

"I made it for Nikki," I replied.

Alexander was making a lot of cooing noises and banging on the tray in front of him.

"Are you eating before you go in to work? Do you want waffles?" Her eyes lifted slowly to meet mine. I was right, she was irritated for some reason. Her eyes were slits, glaring at me.

"I think I'll just have coffee, thanks."

"I normally cook breakfast," Jessica muttered under her breath. I hadn't realized I was stepping on her toes.

Nikki came down the stairs and gave Abby a kiss on the cheek. "Good morning, Pumpkin."

"Morning, Mommy." Abby smiled, waiting for Nikki to look at her.

"Does Alexander eat waffles?" I asked.

"No," Jessica and Nikki answered in unison. They looked at each other and chuckled.

"Well, he's had small pieces before, but we don't give him an entire waffle. Technically, he shouldn't be eating table food at all yet," Nikki said. "But look at him, he's huge. Milk won't keep him satisfied for very long."

I had a lot to learn. I had already made a mental note not to cook breakfast again while Jessica was living with us.

"Oh, Nikki, I made this for you." I placed my hand on the napkin wrapped around the sandwich and slid it across the counter toward her.

"Thank you, baby." She gave me a kiss. "I have to get moving or I'll be late. I'll see you all later."

Nikki kissed Abby and Alexander, then came back and gave me another kiss before grabbing her keys and darting out the front door.

Nikki

My stomach was very unsettled. The thought of setting foot into the office and facing Jack was causing me a lot of anxiety. And the smell of the eggs on that sandwich was making me want to hurl. I pressed the button to let the window down, then unwrapped the paper towel from the sandwich and threw the food out the window. It was a sweet gesture, but I just couldn't eat it. Surely, any little animals in the area would be happy to find it.

After I parked, I sat in the car for some extra minutes before retrieving my phone from my purse. I hadn't called my mother since we returned home, and I needed to just let her know I was back and safe. I had asked about staying with her and Jim after I came back to Tampa, just in case, but needed to let her know my plans had changed.

My mother wasn't happy that Jeff had shown up unannounced in Las Vegas, but she also wasn't surprised when she heard. She was glad we were talking and trying to figure out everything, but once again, she issued a warning to me about his past, and his *playboy* ways. I couldn't help but laugh. In the time I had known him, he never once gave off that type of vibe to me.

I begrudgingly gathered my purse and made my way to the door. I had stalled long enough and had no additional minutes to spare. Before pulling the handle to open the door, I leaned my head back, inhaled a deep breath, held it a few seconds, and then exhaled slowly. I wasn't sure I was ready for this, but I had no choice. Well, I had no choice unless I decided to call out sick or just flat out quit my job while standing right outside of the building.

I made my way up to my desk, set my purse in my drawer, and breathed a sigh of relief that I had avoided Jack so far. Then within seconds I heard his gravelly voice call my name.

"Nikki," Jack said. A shiver ran through me, and my stomach muscles tightened.

My head raised slowly. Super slowly. I didn't want to look him in the eyes, but I knew before the day was over with, it was going to happen. The sooner it was done, the better.

"Yes, Jack?" I answered. I tried to keep my voice quiet.

"I think we need to talk and clear the air." I dropped my head, and my eyes fell to the floor. *Fuck.* I wasn't looking forward to this at all. Not even a little bit.

"I'll be right there." I ran my hands through my hair, gathered and pulled it all back, then secured it loosely with a ponytail holder.

Chapter 17

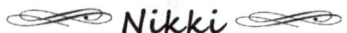

When the clock struck five PM, I couldn't get out of the building fast enough. The day had been painfully long. The bright spot had been going to lunch with everyone.

I walked through the door just before six and was surprised to see Jeff at home already. I had thought for sure he'd get home after me since he went in late. Instead, he stood in the kitchen with Alexander in his arms.

"Look whose home, Alexander," he said. "It's Mommy."

"Hi, babe." I took a few steps in toward the kitchen. "Hi, Alexander." Both of them smiled at me. I could really get used to this greeting every day.

"Mommy!" Abby screamed and ran in to me, wrapping her arms around my legs.

"How are you doing, Abby? How was school?"

"Good. I missed you, Mommy."

"I missed you too, sweetie." I bent down and kissed the top of her head. Her grip didn't loosen. "Are you sure everything is okay, Abby?"

She pulled her arms back. "Yep." And as fast as the reply left her mouth, she took off running back into the living room.

I stepped closer to Jeff, my hands placed on each side of his gorgeous face, and I pulled his full lips down to meet my mouth. I kissed him gently. "I missed *you*."

"I might let you prove it to me later." He winked at me. Alexander fussed and began fidgeting, so I took him from Jeff. That little boy knew the sound of his food truck when he heard me.

"How did you get home so soon? I expected you to be later than me."

"When my three thirty meeting finished, I left. I didn't have anything else on my plate the rest of the afternoon. It was really strange being back in the office, knowing I would be returning daily instead of my routine of traveling so much."

"I'm sure it won't take long to get used to it."

"Yeah, probably." Jeff sat down at the breakfast bar. "I saw that asshole Jason today."

"Please, tell me nothing happened."

"No, it didn't. Pure luck stopped me. I saw him at the end of the hall. I called to him, and he looked like he had seen a ghost. After I took two or three steps in his direction, my name was called, and I got pulled into a conversation. By the time we finished, Jason was nowhere to be seen."

"Jeff, you have to promise me that you won't do anything that will get you in trouble."

"I'm not going to do what I want to, if that's what has you worried. I want to break his nose for putting his hands on you. I want to beat him fucking senseless."

Jessica was doing a really poor job of stifling a laugh as she stirred the delicious-smelling contents in the pot on the stove.

I tilted my head and scrunched my nose at him. "Yeah, that wouldn't be good." I sat Alexander on my lap with the cloth across my legs and began patting him on his back.

"No, but I'd feel better." We all laughed.

"I'm pretty sure you could get your point across just talking to him. You can't do anything that will end up causing you more problems in the long-run. He's not worth it."

 Jeff

Just hearing that weasel Jason's name come out of my mouth and echo in my ears pissed me off all over again. Earlier, at work, it had taken a lot for me not to run down the hall, grab him by his shirt, and slam his pathetic fucking head into the wall. I knew what the consequences would have been, and there was no way I would have done that. But it didn't stop me from daydreaming about kicking his ass. Being in the house with Nikki and the kids was more than enough reason to keep my head.

Jessica was in the kitchen preparing dinner. She has proven to be a really good cook. I knew her parents had wanted her to be a nurse, but she seemed like a natural in the kitchen.

"Now that you've heard about my day, tell me how yours went." Her head fell back, and her eyes closed as she inhaled a deep breath. *Not sounding good so far, and she hasn't even begun to speak,* I thought.

She lifted her head and opened her eyes. "I made it into the office unscathed. I had been at my desk less than a half an hour, then Jack appeared. He approached my desk so quietly, I never even heard him breathe until he called my name. I was caught off guard. I hadn't begun actually working yet, but was contemplating getting some coffee. The sound of his voice startled me so bad my heart raced like it was going to jump out of my chest."

"Did you guys talk?"

"Yeah, we did. He apologized for his brother's belligerence, and he swore he had nothing to do with it. He said he had invited Jason to join us, but had absolutely no idea he was going to pounce on me like that."

"In all fairness, Nikki, he may not have," Jessica said. "From what you said, I thought your boss was an innocent bystander and just happened to be related to the ranting fool."

"You're probably right," Nikki replied.

We both smiled at Jessica as she left the room to set the table in the dining room. "He's probably telling the truth, you know," I said.

"Yeah, true. But still, Jack had heard some of the crap Jason was saying before. He wasn't shocked by the words; he was just shocked that Jason was saying them to me."

"Did he say anything else?" I asked.

"He asked me not to associate what his brother said with him, yada, yada, yada, blah, blah, blah. Then we talked about nothing really for about fifteen more minutes before he told me a supervisor's job was going to be opening up in the next month. He wants me to give serious consideration to applying for it." She rolled her eyes, then stood, hoisting Alexander up onto her hip.

"That's good. It doesn't sound like it went bad."

"No, it didn't. Oh, I had told Candace and Georgia I had a run-in with Jason. I never told them details because I didn't have time. They both apologized for leaving so early that night. They thought if they had stayed, maybe that wouldn't have happened. I told them it wasn't their fault. Jason came in with the intention of saying what he said, and they couldn't have stopped him. Jack couldn't even get him to shut up."

"Then that sorry piece of shit put his hands on you." My blood began to boil all over again just thinking about his nasty-ass, chapped lips touching hers after suggesting they hook up. *Motherfucker*. He caused all of this bullshit over nothing but lies. And he had the fucking audacity to suggest that Nikki was an afterthought to me, fucking second best to that bitch wife of his, Blake. Even saying he was second to me, in Blake's opinion. Every muscle in my body tensed and my jaw tightened.

I inhaled deeply and walked over beside Nikki and ran my fingers through the length of her hair. "Let it go, Jeff. He's not worth any of your time or energy." The voice of reason, but I wasn't feeling terribly reasonable.

"I need to ask you about something later." She looked up at me with those huge, doe-like brown eyes.

"We can talk now if you want," she said. I knew how much she hated waiting. Her mind had a tendency to work overtime to make up ridiculous shit when she had to wait to find out what we were going to talk about.

"It's not that big of a deal; it can wait."

****

Dinner was amazing.

After watching a couple of cartoons, Nikki told Abby it was time for bed. Alexander fell asleep while we sat on the sofa. Jessica had gone up to her room to watch television instead of staying downstairs with us. We could hear her talking and laughing, and we were pretty sure she was on her phone talking to the guy she met in Las Vegas.

Once the kids were all tucked in, we made our way into our bedroom to brush our teeth.

"You said a couple things in Vegas that have really been bugging me," I said. I put toothpaste on my brush.

"What was that?" Nikki asked with her toothbrush hanging out of her mouth. She looked adorable with toothpaste nearly dribbling down her chin.

"You made a comment about protecting your heart. What did you mean when you said that?" I finished brushing, then I rinsed my mouth and sat on the tub surround. I watched her rinse her mouth, then pat it dry with her washcloth. "Well," she said. She walked out into the bedroom and dug around in my dresser drawer to find a T-shirt. I walked out and sat on the bench at the foot of the bed. Once she had what she was looking for, she removed her clothes and slipped the shirt over her head, letting it glide down her sexy body.

"Like what my mom went through all those years. Remember I told you about that, with my dad? I want to make sure I don't go through the same type of thing." Nikki sat on the bench next to me and intertwined her fingers with mine. She rehashed stories her mom had told her about the arguments. What really had stood out to her were the dirty looks she remembered seeing them exchange, the last big fight, and her dad abandoning her and her brother.

"At the time, I thought if I left here, instead of facing you, it would lessen the impact of my heartbreak. Instead, it made me feel really guilty, on top of being sad. I wondered if I had done the right thing, or made things worse. Not only did I leave you, I took Alexander from you. That wasn't fair. I'll never do that again, no matter what happens with us."

"You automatically convicted me and I was presumed guilty. I had no chance to explain or tell you it wasn't true. You took away my ability to defend myself, and I had no say in the matter whatsoever." Before she could reply, I turned slightly toward her, grabbed a handful of her hair, and pulled her to me until our mouths met. My tongue collided with hers. That minty toothpaste taste with a hint of her. It was heavenly.

"This thing between us, this is real. This isn't a game."

"I know," she whispered. She laid her head on my shoulder and wrapped her arm around my back at the waist.

"I'm not your father, Nikki. We all aren't cut from the same cloth. You do realize that, right? Not all men would do what he did to you and Gary."

"Yeah, I know. But I couldn't shut off the thought of that happening. There are so many times when I'm sitting on the couch or at my desk at work that I ask myself when the wheels will fall off of our relationship. Will you cheat on me? Will you leave me?"

"Doll, maybe you need to get counseling. I'm not saying that to be funny. I just don't think it's very mentally healthy to keep mulling over thoughts like that, though. You have to find a way to let that kind of thinking go."

"You're right. I've thought about going to talk to my dad. I have some questions I really want to know the answers to, and he's the only person who can provide the answers."

"Then you should do that. And don't wait for months to pass. Maybe you can go see him next week sometime. Now that I'm home in the evenings, just go after work one day and have a nice long talk with him. Whatever you need to do to help you, and not second guess me, I support you one hundred percent."

"Thanks, baby. I don't want to keep having these crazy thoughts. I'll give him a call before the end of this week and set something up," she said, then yawned.

"In the bed with you." I stood and held out my hand to pull her up. Once she was standing in front of me, my arms wrapped around her waist and I held her tight to me.

"I thought I was going to show you how much I missed you." Our eyes were fixed on each other.

"Not tonight; you need your sleep. We have plenty of time for that. And I'm happy just holding you in my arms tonight." I kissed her forehead. "I love you, baby doll. Forever."

"I love you too, Jeff."

My mouth descended on hers. She was everything I'd always wanted or needed in a woman.

We loosened our hold on each other, and we both climbed in the bed, her on her side, and me on mine. I pulled her body close to mine so her back was flush against my chest and wrapped my arms around her waist, holding her tight.

"You do know we're connected for life, right? No matter how hard you try, you can't get rid of me."

"I don't want to get rid of you, ever."

"Good. I love you more than my next breath; life is nothing without you."

Her body relaxed into mine, and I showered her neck and shoulder with light kisses.

Chapter 18

 Jeff

The alarm clock made its ghastly noise, signaling it was time for me to get up. I was surprised to find that Nikki wasn't in the bed. I trudged into the bathroom to brush my teeth and shower. The enthusiasm from the day before had long gone away. Today, I had to be in the office by eight o'clock for a client meeting.

I reached the top of the stairs to make my way down to the kitchen, and I could hear laughter. I loved that sound.

"Good morning," I said as my foot came off of the last step onto the kitchen floor.

"Good morning," Jessica said.

Abby ran over to me and hugged my legs. "Good morning, Daddy Jeff." She released me and returned to her seat, grabbed her spoon, and shoved a huge amount of oatmeal in her mouth. I didn't think kids even liked oatmeal.

"Well, look at you," Nikki said. Her eyes scanned me from the top of my head down to my feet, then back up until our eyes met. Her smile was like a ray of sunshine.

"Eh, no biggie. It's just a suit." I could see that heated, lustful look in her eyes. It was times like this that made me wish I was a billionaire and didn't have to work at all.

"And a mighty fine suit it is, Mr. Carrington," she purred.

Nikki

He couldn't have looked any more handsome if he tried. He stood in the kitchen looking like my dream come true. My husband.

His arms were testing the strength of the fabric and stitching. If he flexed his muscles, I was sure he could rip out of that jacket like the Hulk. My sex clenched at the thought.

"Thank you, Mrs. Carrington."

I licked my lower lip, biting it, sucking it gently into my mouth. I'd give anything to have five minutes to rip his slacks down and suck him into my mouth, but I knew we didn't even have that much spare time. He had to go into the office early.

"Do you have any plans for lunch today?" Jeff asked.

"Nope, no plans."

"I'll call you before I come by."

"Really, you'll have time to come see me?" That was a surprise. I hadn't even given any thought to us being able to meet for lunch.

"Sure. I have some free time between eleven thirty and one, so be ready."

"I'll be ready."

He gave Alexander a pat on the head, Abby a kiss on the cheek, then leaned in and kissed my forehead, holding his lips pressed to my skin longer than normal. I inhaled, taking the scent of his cologne into my lungs. His fingers weaved into my hair until they rubbed on my scalp.

"I'll see you later." He grabbed his keys and rushed out the door.

Jessica helped me get Abby ready to go to day care. I was going to drop her off on my way to work. Alexander was fed and happy. Each morning, I couldn't help but wonder just how much longer we'd keep Jessica. I was more than capable of taking care of the kids. And Alexander could certainly go to daycare with Abby. They had taken such great care of Abby when she was a baby, and everyone I knew then still worked there. I trusted them. I knew Jeff and I needed to figure this out.

"Abby, are you almost ready?" I asked.

"Almost, Mommy."

She was sitting on the ground, struggling to get her shoes tied. "Do you need help?"

"No, I'm doing it." Her little mouth was turned down at the corners, and her eyes scrunched, while her little fingers fumbled and twisted the shoe strings. Her other pair of shoes had Velcro, and they were so much easier for her to put on, but she insisted on wearing these. She was so headstrong about things.

"We have to go, baby. I'll give you two more minutes, then I'll have to help you so we aren't late."

"Okay."

She was working furiously, twisting and wrapping. "I'm done."

"Okay, grab your lunch, and let's go." I picked up my purse and keys. "See you later, Jessica. Bye, Alexander." I gave him a kiss on his warm, chubby, pink cheek.

Abby grabbed her lunch from the counter, then gave Alexander a hug and a big wet kiss. "Bye, baby." She gave a quick wave to Jessica. "Bye, Miss Jessi."

I walked into work with a few minutes to spare. I grabbed my mug and headed down to the break area to get a cup of coffee. I was surprised to see Candace and Georgia in there. "Good morning, Ladies."

"Hey, Nikki. How are you?"

Their inquiring minds wanted to know the details of the run-in with Jason. I told them the story about what had happened at happy hour after they had left that Thursday night. I left out some of the details. I didn't want them to know everything. And honestly, I didn't want to relive it all again. They both apologized, again, for leaving so early that night. I told them that Jack and I had talked yesterday. Again, leaving out a lot of the details, but they got the gist of it.

"Is everything okay now? I mean, between you and Jeff?" Georgia asked. Her hand stroked down my arm.

"Yeah, everything is fine; thanks for asking."

"That's good to hear," Georgia said.

What are you doing for lunch today?" Candace asked.

"Jeff is going to come by, and we're going to lunch together."

"Jeff?" Candace asked. The two of them stared at me.

"Oh, yeah, I forgot to tell you that. He isn't traveling any more like he had been. So he's working at the office in town. He's only about fifteen minutes from here."

"That's nice. So I guess no more happy hours or lunch dates," Georgia said. Her voice had quieted to a near whisper.

"It's not like that. I'll still be going to happy hours. Well, I don't know, after the last one…" We all chuckled. "I'm sure I'll go, just maybe not so frequently. And we definitely will still be going to lunch together, just not today."

"I have to go get some work done. We can chat some more later this afternoon; maybe during our after-lunch coffee time," Candace said.

"Sounds like a plan. I'll talk to you both later."

I still had a lot of work to catch up on. There were no interruptions after I got logged in. It surprised me that Jack hadn't come by my desk, but I was very happy that he hadn't. I didn't want to discuss anything to do with that night again. Not with him, not with anyone.

A smile crossed my face when I heard my phone chime. I knew that was Jeff texting me. I pulled my phone out of my purse and confirmed it.

Jeff: *Ready? I'll be there in 10*

I quickly replied to him.

Me: *I'll be downstairs waiting*

I took a few minutes to go to the restroom and check my hair. I was standing at the curb waiting for him when he pulled up. I quickly climbed into the seat of his car and closed the door behind me, then turned to him and smiled.

"So what's on the menu for lunch?"

He gave me a quick, sly glance. "You."

"What?" Tingles raced through me, and my heart rate increased.

"You heard me." He glanced at me again out of the corner of his eye.

"Um, so we're not getting any food?" I was starving.

"We'll have time to stop somewhere quick after, but first, I need to have a taste of my favorite dish. You."

I was completely flabbergasted.

"Where are we going to go? There are laws against sex in public, you know." I laughed, but wasn't amused. I didn't want to go through the embarrassment of getting hauled off to jail for a lunchtime quickie.

Jeff

"I have the perfect spot. Relax."

I could tell she was shitting a brick. It was my lunch, my meal of choice, and I chose to eat her. I'd make sure she got some food before taking her back.

We pulled into the parking lot and I parked in the very back tree-lined row of spaces. Her mouth fell open. I laughed. The look on her face was priceless.

"You're kidding me, right?" she asked.

"Not at all. Get in the back seat."

"How did you come up with this place?"

"Don't ask, doll, just hurry up." I was laughing hysterically. The look on her face was priceless, and almost worth just parking here. I had no intention of telling her one of my new office mates had told me a couple of weeks ago he had brought a woman here for a quickie. A state park seemed like a huge risk, but there were so many parking lots. It was easy to find a space where no one else was parked, especially at that time of day.

She did as I asked. She sat in the backseat with her back against the door and her legs turned in toward me. Her arms were crossed over her perfect breasts. I joined her, then inched her skirt up her thighs. She lifted her ass so I could press it up around her waist. Her expression never changed. But it was going to.

"Perfect, baby, perfect," I moaned. I dipped my head and inhaled her beautiful scent. She wanted me; I could smell it.

My fingers pushed her panties to the side, exposing her glistening pussy to me. I ran my fingers along her slit, letting them slide in between her slick lips. "Mmm, nice and wet."

Her arms dropped to her sides from the I'm-pissed-off-and-I-refuse-to-like-it position across her breasts. My cock was rock hard, straining to get free of my pants. But I wasn't going to fuck her. Not here. She'd get that later tonight.

I inhaled her scent one more time before I licked my tongue between her swollen labia. Tasting her was divine. I could never get enough of her. I reached my arms underneath her thighs and held her at her waist, then pulled her closer to me, seating her hot sex perfectly on my tongue. I wanted her to ride my mouth with my tongue buried deep in her sweet hole.

"Damn, baby," she moaned.

I felt like it was a strained moan. I wanted her to appreciate being here with me as much as I appreciated her. I slid two fingers inside her and sucked her clit into my mouth. My tongue lashed around her hard bud like I was gargling a marble. Her legs clamped tight around my head. "Fuck, baby. Damn!" she cried out.

My fingers pounded inside her while my mouth kept working her clit. "Mmm," I moaned.

She held my hair in her hands and pressed her pussy tighter into my face. She was close. So close.

A third finger found its way inside her, while I used my thumb to apply pressure to her beautiful, puckered, saliva-covered ass. She spread her legs as wide as she could and held my hand tight to her snatch while she humped me. With one thumb applying pressure to her ass knot, and the other thumb strumming her clit, she broke. "Damn it, baby. Fuck!"

I didn't let up on the pressure. I wanted to see how long she could come before begging me to stop. "Keep coming, baby," I said.

When it looked like she was close to coming down, I used my mouth to reapply pressure and wind her back up. God, I loved that she was able to come like that.

"Shit, baby, stop. Please stop," she begged.

I didn't want this to end. My cock was so hard, I knew I'd have blue balls the rest of the afternoon, but it was worth it. She was so worth it.

I pulled my fingers from her juicy cunt and licked them clean while she watched me. "You taste so fucking good, Nikki. You're the best lunch ever."

Chapter 19

 *Nikki*

Jeff dropped me off in front of my building with a sated, sopping-wet pussy, and a bag of Chick-fil-A fries. I felt like I had a silly grin plastered across my face. I wanted to go to lunch with him every day. *Damn.*

I stopped in the bathroom to make sure my hair looked okay, and to wipe away some of the excess wetness before I went to my desk. By the time I got to my desk, it was one fifteen, and Jack was standing there waiting for me with a scowl on his face. There wasn't anything he could say right now that could bring me down, though.

"Nikki," Jack said. "I have something I need your help with. Can you come in my office in five minutes?"

"Sure," I replied. I was floating. I planned to ride cloud nine right down the hallway and into his office.

He walked back toward his office. I put all of my belongings in my drawer, grabbed a notepad and pen, and then made my way down there right behind him. I knocked on his door and was told to come in.

"Please, sit down," he said.

I sat in the chair he pointed to and felt my inflamed lips remind me that my husband had just worked me over. My sex clenched when my hips rolled in the chair.

"I need you to run a report for me," Jack said. *Really? A report?* I hadn't run a report for him in months. We had adhoc report writers. Why wasn't he telling one of them what he needed? "I need this in thirty minutes, and there can't be any mistakes, Nikki."

"Okay, let me know what you need."

"This report will be for specific accounts and it will be shared with Senior Management. If they're satisfied with the output, I'll need you to run it run every morning so we can keep an eye on the business details." He had my attention. I knew this report was a high priority for someone above him. He had never asked me to run a report like this for him before. When I received all of the specifications from him, I went back to my desk and began setting up the SQL to pull the data he needed.

After verifying the output on the report, I took it down to Jack, then returned to my desk. My phone chimed. I had hoped it was Jeff. I pulled it from my purse.

Jeff: *I still taste you, and smell you on my fingers.*

Me: *I still feel your fingers and tongue in me ;)*

Jeff: *You'll feel more than that in you later tonight*

Me: *I can't wait. Mmm*

"Am I interrupting a moment?" Candace asked.

My eyes opened and saw her smiling at me across the top of my cubical wall. "Um, no, you aren't," I replied.

"Want to come down to get some coffee?"

"Sure." I grabbed my mug and put my phone back in my purse. We walked down to the break room chatting about a lot of nothing.

"I was beginning to wonder about you two," Georgia said.

Candace and I filled our cups with coffee and added creamer, then went to sit down at a small table in the room.

"How was lunch?" Georgia asked.

"It was magnificent."

"Hmm, I've never heard of lunch described that way. What did you eat?"

"Chick-fil-A fries."

"Okay, I know you love your fries, but magnificent?" Candace and Georgia both looked at me with an eyebrow raised.

"Trust me, it was a magnificent lunch," I said. I winked at them.

"Oh. Ohhh, I get it," Georgia said, smirking.

 Jeff

I sat at my desk and in meetings all afternoon with a *cat-that-ate-the-canary* grin on my face, according to Connor. Eating Nikki for lunch had been a delicious appetizer. I planned to have her completely later this evening, after we got the kids to bed. I held my fingers under my nose as I drove home.

I walked in the house and straight to the kitchen, where Nikki and Jessica were talking. Nikki was sitting on a stool at the breakfast bar, holding Alexander, who looked very tired. She looked in my direction, and our eyes met.

"Hi, babe," Nikki said. Jessica said hi, then took my boy from Nikki. I heard Abby's counting game on and guessed she was glued to the television.

"Hello, Ladies," I answered. Jessica smiled over her shoulder as she walked into the living room.

"What's with that sinister smile?" Nikki asked.

I walked over and stood behind her. With my left hand on her shoulder, I wrapped my right hand across her mouth, making sure my index finger was just below her nose. I leaned down and whispered in her ear, "Do you smell that, baby?" I had washed my hands several times in the afternoon, yet her mouth-watering scent lingered.

She inhaled deep. "Yeah, I do."

"That was my lunch today. Doesn't it smell delicious?"

"It does." I cupped her chin with my left hand and pressed my finger into her mouth. She was so responsive to me. She sucked on my finger, raising her hands to mine, wrapping them around my fist. She sucked and licked around my finger as if she were sucking my cock.

"I've been finding the cleverest ways to smell you all afternoon. I need you, baby. I need to feel you."

"Mmm," she moaned. I pressed my hardness into her back. My pants had become uncomfortably tight, like they had at least once earlier in the day, thinking about her. I felt like I could have shot my load in my trousers. I wanted her.

She kept sucking, her head laid back against my stomach and her eyes closed, moaning quietly. She was pulling my finger as deep as she could get it into her throat.

I lowered my head and kissed her forehead, and, at the same time, I pulled my finger from her lips.

"Upstairs, baby. Now."

Chapter 20

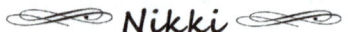 Nikki

The report I created for Jack had been approved. I had to run it every morning and have it delivered to him by ten am. He had also asked me to train some guy named Michael, a newly hired marketing tactician. I didn't understand what Jack was doing. I wasn't learning anyone else's job, yet I was teaching someone else how to do mine. And this was the second person I would have taught to replace me. The skeptic in me couldn't help but wonder if Jack was trying to set me up to be let go. I knew he had told me about the supervisor's role, but nothing else had been said since that initial discussion.

"Good morning, Nikki." I looked up and saw a good-looking, thin, short, blond man, probably in his early twenties, standing beside my desk with Jack.

I sat up and leaned back in my chair. "Good morning."

"Nikki, this is Michael Lightner. He'll be sitting with you for the next few days to learn what you do."

"Hi, Michael," I said. I graciously offered my hand out to shake his. "Grab a chair from one of the empty cubicles, and we can get started."

He looked around like finding a chair was the most difficult task he had been given in life. I fought the urge to shake my head when he walked around the corner.

"I'll leave the two of you alone. Please, don't forget my report," Jack said.

"I won't forget." I was relieved to see the distance increase between the backside of him and me. This day wasn't getting off to a good start.

Michael had an intense look on his face as he pushed the chair around the corner to my desk.

"Do you drink coffee, Michael?"

"Yes, I do. And please, call me Mike. My mom used to call me Michael when I was in trouble."

"Okay, Mike. Let's go get a cup of coffee, then we can get started."

I introduced Mike to the few people down in the break room. When we left, I took him on a quick tour, showing him where the restroom was, and the conference rooms. Then we returned to my desk and addressed the first priority -- Jack's report. When we walked down to Jack's office, I let Mike take it in to him while I stood in the doorway. Jack seemed thrilled that I had gotten it to him on time and that I had begun delegating to Mike.

With Mike being new, I invited him to go to lunch with Candace, Georgia, Robert, and me. I'd hoped Tristan would join us, but he and his girlfriend had plans already.

Mike was introduced to the best pizza restaurant in Tampa, in my opinion. We all sat and chatted while we ate, then I excused myself for a couple of minutes.

I'd made up my mind while I was getting ready for work that I was going to call my father on a break. I hadn't talked to him in months. The last time was shortly after we had returned from our honeymoon. He had never seen Alexander, and his only time seeing Abby was at the wedding while she zipped around the reception hall.

"Hello?"

"Daddy?" I asked.

"Nikki? Is that you?" I heard my dad's voice crack.

"It's me, Daddy. How are you doing?"

"Ah, you know. I'm getting older, and the bones creak a little more." He laughed. "How are things going with you? How's that husband of yours treating you?"

"Things are really good with Jeff; he treats me great."

"I'm glad to hear that. He seemed like a really good guy, Nikki."

"He is." I swallowed hard. "Daddy, I want to come by and see you. Are you going to be home next week, maybe Monday?"

"You can come by anytime you want. I'll be here. I'm not working anymore."

"Oh, you're retired? Aren't you a little young for that?"

"No, I'm on permanent disability. I can't work anymore. We can talk about that when you come by. I'm looking forward to seeing you."

"Me too. I have to get back to work now, but I'll be over on Monday after work."

"Bye, Nikki; thanks for calling me."

"Bye, Daddy."

I sensed a sadness in my dad's voice while we talked. I really wanted to go see him today to make sure he was okay, but decided against it. I'd stick with the plan and go on Monday.

 *Jeff*

Connor and I walked back inside the building, and that was when I saw him. That elusive, filthy, rat bastard, Jason.

"I'll talk to you later, Connor."

After I got two steps away from Connor, he called out behind me, "Jeff, don't do anything crazy."

I waved at him over my back. I was in control, and just hoped Jason didn't say or do anything that would cause me to lose that. Adrenaline surged through me, and my heart raced as I got closer to him. He didn't even see me as I stepped within a foot of his sorry, soft body. It was perfect timing; his scummy buddy had just walked away.

"Jason," I said.

"Oh, hey, Jeff," he said. "What's going on?"

"We need to talk, but you already knew that, didn't you?"

"Um, I don't know what you're talking about."

"Like hell you don't, you snake," I snarled. "Outside, now. I'm not doing this here in the lobby."

"I need to, um, get to a meeting."

"Nice try. Are you going to walk outside or am I going to help you find the door?"

"Fine. Asshole." I laughed. I'm the asshole. This guy was living in an alternate universe if he didn't realize he was the biggest asshole here.

Chapter 21

"Sweetheart, I'm home." I laughed when I heard Nikki and Jessica chuckle.

"Hi, baby, how was your day?" Nikki asked. She walked into the foyer with Alexander in her arms. I took my little guy from her.

"It was just great," I said. "How was yours?"

"Interesting. Disheartening."

"What happened?" I followed her as we walked into the kitchen.

"Hey, Jessica. Hi, Abby."

Abby turned to look at me, gave me a little wave, and then she redirected her attention back to her coloring book she had on the table.

"I have a new person to train how to do my job. I don't know what Jack's up to, but something about this seems kind of fishy to me." I sat down at the breakfast bar.

"Well, babe, if he was talking to you about being a supervisor, someone would need to back-fill your position, right?"

"Yeah, that's true, but I'm not doing anything to prepare to move into a new position. I'm just working myself out of a job by training others." Nikki was standing on the opposite side of the breakfast bar. She leaned over at the hips and rested her elbows on the counter surface and placed her chin in her hands. I couldn't help but notice her inviting cleavage was exposed to me.

"I'd bet that's not true. Jack needs to know your job can be done and done well, then he can work with you to get you ready for the new job. If he took you now, without training a replacement, there's a lot of work that wouldn't get done."

"I guess you're right. I wish he'd talk to me and explain things better." She stood up straight, then reached up in the cupboard to retrieve a glass.

I shifted Alexander from one arm to the other.

"Oh, and I talked to my dad. I'm going to stop by on Monday after work, if that's okay with you."

"Of course it is. Do you want me to come over with you?"

"No, um, not this time. I want to talk to him alone first. But I'd like you and the kids to come over for sure another time."

"Okay, just let me know."

Nikki poured a glass of orange juice and set it on the counter in front of me. How thoughtful of her, but she forgot the shot of gin.

"I was debating whether to tell you what happened with me today, but what the hell. I may as well, right?"

"Yeah, tell me."

"I had a *chat* with your friend Jason."

"You didn't."

"Oh, I did. I saw him in the lobby when I came back from lunch with Connor. I walked right up to within inches of him and called his name. He reluctantly went outside with me and we talked."

I looked up at Jessica. After we made eye contact, I looked at Abby. She helped Abby gather her crayons and book, then they moved into the living room.

"Jeff, you didn't ..."

"I didn't put my hands on him, if that's what you're worried about. I wanted to, but I didn't," I said. "I wanted him to tell me why in the hell he would tell you all of those lies."

"What did he say?"

"Of course, at first, he didn't have an excuse. Then he told me, a few days after the picnic, Blake let him know she didn't love him. She never had."

"Oh my God, that had to have been devastating to hear."

"He also said Blake told him she loved *me*. He had been trying to figure out how he could get back at me. I didn't do anything. But he became more and more furious when he thought back to that day, and how Blake was acting around me."

"I can see where he's coming from."

"Nikki, please, don't start. I made it perfectly clear that if Blake was out of town, or cheating on him, she wasn't with me, and I have absolutely no interest in her. I also told him he better not ever again, as long as he lives, ever think that you are second fiddle to anyone. You're number one to me, period. Forever."

Nikki covered her mouth and snickered. "What did he say? How did he react?"

"He stood there and looked terrified. He knew I wanted to rip him apart." I took a small drink of my juice. "The funniest was when I said something about him putting his hands on you. Every single bit of pigmentation faded from his face, I swear. You would have been proud of me though. As much as I wanted to rip his heart from his chest, I didn't even poke him or point in his face."

Nikki giggled and clapped her hands. "That's so awesome, baby. I am so proud of you for keeping your cool. Thank you for sticking up for me."

"Are you kidding me? I'd do anything for you. And I'll make sure a scumbag like him never thinks about doing anything like that to you, or anyone else, ever again."

****

After the kids went to sleep, I decided it was time to get Nikki to tell me her honest feelings about the second thing that really got under my skin in Las Vegas. Her statement had been repeating in my mind ever since I had first heard the words come out of her mouth, and it was really bothering me.

"Baby doll, come sit closer to me." We were downstairs in the living room, alone, sitting on the couch. She was over by the lamp. She scooted over and wedged herself close to me, my arm wrapped around her shoulder.

"I'm going to ask you a question, and I want an honest answer. Don't try to tell me what you think I want to hear. Just please, tell me the truth. Okay?" I said.

"Yeah, sure."

"I heard you say, not just once, but twice, while we were in Las Vegas that this was my house." Her breath hitched at my words. "Is that the way you feel? That this house is not ours? You still see it as just mine?"

"I didn't realize I said that."

"Well, see, I'm not sure I believe that's the truth. I'm pretty sure you've referred to this house as mine, not ours, on at least one other occasion before we were married. Am I wrong?"

"Well ..."

"Baby, am I wrong?"

"No, you're not wrong."

"So you really don't look at this house as ours, but as mine?"

"Since you want me to be completely honest, I want to see it as *ours*, but it doesn't feel like that to me. I've only been able to make a couple simple little additions, like the key hooks by the front door, and the tablecloths in the kitchen and dining room. Everything else was here before I moved in. A house that's mine, I can feel free to paint the walls and decorate." She sighed.

"I guess I've been a bit stubborn, but not because I wanted you to feel like this wasn't your house too. I've gotten so used to the way things are. Why fix something if it isn't broken, right?"

Nikki sat up and turned to face me. "Does that mean I can make some changes, and paint?"

"I'll do better than that for you. But you have to give me some time."

She let her body mold against mine and leaned her head back so she was looking up at me. "I can wait. That will give me some time to figure out exactly what I want to do. I think I'm going to start in the kitchen. I'm so excited! I promise, I won't turn it into a girly dollhouse."

Chapter 22

The weekend flew by in a blur, and the workweek was upon us again. I moved the extra seat that Mike would be sitting in so it was situated in front of my computer. I had a surprise for him today. It was his turn to be hands-on. We had spent a couple of days together last week with him watching me, and I had until Wednesday to finish my training with him. The sooner he was able to experience the work flow and computer system, the better off he would be. Everything I had told him, and showed him, would make more sense.

As hard as I tried to think of nothing else except work, my thoughts kept wandering to the visit I was supposed to have with my dad after work. I was having a hard time staying focused. I kept rearranging the personal things on my desk. I glanced at the clock and noticed it was nine thirty. Mike was running late.

I quickly ran the report for Jack and delivered it to his assistant, then returned to my desk. I was disappointed because I had planned for Mike to do it on his own.

"Good morning," Mike said. He startled me. It had to have been visible that I jumped at the sound of his voice. "Sorry I'm late, I had a meeting with my former manager this morning."

"Hi, Mike, no worries. I got Jack's report to him already. Coffee?"

"Definitely," he replied. "Um, what are you doing? Is that my seat?" He had his hand on my chair, while pointing to the empty seat in front of the computer.

"Yeah, that's yours."

****

The work day finally ended, and, after getting to my car, I sat there for several minutes contemplating the conversation I'd have with my dad. My insides were quivering like Jell-O. I wasn't sure what to expect from him when I asked the questions that were burning in my mind. Would he get upset? Would he shut down on me and refuse to answer?

I took in a deep breath, exhaled slowly, and then started my car. My thoughts were everywhere except on the task at hand, driving. I completely missed a stop sign. I drove right through it, and just missed hitting a car that had the right of way through the intersection. At least that was what the police officer told me when he handed me my ticket. I shook my head. I really didn't want to tell Jeff about the near miss. But our pact of no lies and no secrets wasn't selective.

I'd made it in one piece to my dad's house and parked in the street. I sat in the car with my hands gripping the steering wheel, rocking back and forth, giving myself a silent pep talk. My breaths were short. I looked at the front door, then at the clock on the dash. I had sat there for almost ten minutes. "Get out of the car; go talk to him," I said to myself.

I had never been inside my dad's house. When we met after my wedding, it had been in a park. I thought that was the best place. It was in the open on neutral territory, and if our conversation had taken a turn for the worse, we could have parted ways easily. But we had a nice conversation that day. I wasn't sure this one would be the same with the agenda I had, though.

Somehow, I managed to walk up to the door on wobbly legs, and ring the doorbell. A woman opened the door.

"Hi, you must be Nikki. Wow, your father sure described you perfectly. You're beautiful, just like he said."

"Thank you. Yes, I'm Nikki. Is Daddy here?"

"Where are my manners? Yes, he's here. Come on in." I stepped into the house and felt like my breath had been sucked from my body. I wanted to gasp, but feared taking in any more air than necessary would damage my lungs in some way. "My name in Sharon. I've been living with your dad for almost six years now. Excuse the house, I haven't had a chance to clean in a few days. I work two jobs and, well, your dad just can't do much to help me out anymore."

"It's nice to meet you, Sharon." I shook her hand. "Why? Why can't Daddy help out?"

"I'll let him tell you. It's better if you hear everything from him. Come on, he's in the back room."

The house had a pungent, sour-smelling odor as we walked down the filthy hall. The carpet looked like it was months overdue for vacuuming. I took shallow breaths, but it did nothing to help minimize the smell infiltrating my nose.

"Here he is." She pointed into the room. "Sweetheart, look who it is?"

Daddy turned to face me. It took everything in my power not to cry.

The strong man I had known, my father, was sitting before me in a wheelchair. He'd had a belly before he left us, when I was in high school, but had gotten himself in better shape when I saw him at my wedding. Now, my heart ached at the sight of him sitting there. He looked so many years older than he had just a few months ago. And his body had taken a turn for the worse. He looked weak and frail. He had to have been at least twenty-five pounds lighter. He didn't even look like my dad. And he wore glasses. My dad had never worn glasses before. He'd always had perfect vision.

"Nikki, thanks for coming over. Have a seat. It's so good to see you."

I glanced down at the clothes-covered couch. Then looked at a chair on the other side of my dad, with clothes piled high on it, too.

"You can just move some of those clothes. Sorry about that. Sharon has her hands full and just hasn't had a chance to get them put away yet."

"It's okay, I understand." I reached to pick up the pile of clothes from the chair.

"I can get those, Nikki, sorry about that."

"Don't apologize. I got it, thanks." I relocated them to the couch to join all of the other piles. Sharon patted my shoulder just before she left the room. "How are you doing, Daddy?" My voice cracked. I felt like I was going to lose the battle with my emotions before I left his house.

"I'm making out okay. I have my good days and my bad days." Daddy's voice was low and gravelly; it was no longer the booming voice I had grown used to during my childhood.

My eyes wandered around the small, cluttered room. The television was small, and was set only a few feet from my dad. The couch was way too big for the room. It took up a lot of space. There were knick-knacks everywhere. There was potential for the room to be quite a nice space, but it needed a thorough cleaning. And maybe to lose a few of those clown figurines -- like all of them.

"Daddy, what happened?" I asked. My chest tightened, and I clasped my fingers together. I was sitting on the edge of the chair, leaning slightly forward.

"I guess it was about a week or two after we met in the park, I had a stroke." I gasped. I couldn't believe he hadn't told me. "That one wasn't that bad, but the next one, a couple of weeks later, was a doozy."

"Why didn't you say anything to me?" A tear slid down my face. It saddened me to think my father had gone through that.

"I didn't want to be a bother to anyone. It's been rough, and really depressing. Do you have any idea how hard it is to go from being able to take care of myself to depending on someone to do everything for me?" His eyes were shiny with tears. "Sharon's been taking real good care of me, though, and we thought after the first stroke I'd get back to normal. It was after the second stroke …" he said. His voiced became unsteady. "That was when I was told I couldn't work anymore and she took on a second job. We've been hoping my strength would come back, but so far, it hasn't. And my memory isn't the greatest anymore." A single tear slid down his face, following the crease near his nose.

"Oh, Daddy," I said. I walked over to him, leaned down, and wrapped my arms around his neck. He hugged me back. My fight to hold back my own tears was lost.

"Don't worry about me. I'm doing fine, now. The doctors told me just last week everything was looking good. I just need to gain some weight back and I'll be good as new." He chuckled. I didn't believe him, but smiled anyway.

I sat back down in the chair. My heart broke for Sharon and Daddy. They had been going through so much for months and never said a word to anyone. I felt bad for not calling him, or offering to come over sooner. I had spent so much time with Jeff's mom, and my mom, that I completely neglected trying to work on my relationship with my own father.

"How's your family doing?" Daddy asked me.

"They're all doing really well. Everything is great between me and Jeff. We just hit a bad patch, but we're fine now. And the kids are doing great."

"Kids? I thought you just had the daughter."

"I guess I didn't tell you. I was four months pregnant when I got married. Jeff and I have a son. He's almost four months old."

"Wow. Isn't that something? Well, congratulations. I'd sure love to see the grandbabies one of these days."

"I'll bring them over, or maybe you can come over to our house. I'd like them to get to know you, their grandfather." I sat back in the chair.

"I meant to ask you, Daddy, speaking of kids ... I know your girlfriend was pregnant when you and Mom split up. Do I have a brother or a sister? I never did find out."

"You have a sister. She looks a lot like you. Amanda -- that's her name. She just turned twelve. She's smart as a whip and has a sassy mouth. I guess it's her age."

"I'd like to meet her someday."

"I think that would be a great idea. I'd love for you to get to know her. Gary too."

"Well, I can't speak for Gary. I wouldn't get my hopes up too high on him, but I can say something to him about it." We sat in silence. It was an awkward lull in our conversation where I tried to muster up the courage to ask what I had come for.

"So what's really brought you by, Nikki? Something on your mind?"

"I don't want to upset you." I noticed I had begun scratching and digging at my arm.

"Nonsense. I know you have something bugging you." He pointed at my arms. "You've had that habit since you were a little girl. Always scratching yourself when you get nervous."

We both laughed.

"I want to know some things, if you'll tell me. I think ..." I swallowed hard. I was not having much luck delivering the question the way I had rehearsed it in my mind.

"What? What's going on?"

"I guess ... I just want to know," I shifted in my seat and crossed my legs at my knees. "When you left us, why didn't you ever try to stay in touch with me and Gary?"

He dropped his head, and raised a hand up to hold his forehead in his fingers. I watched as his shoulders lifted and fell. He was barely audible, but I heard his soft sobs.

"Daddy?" I didn't want to be the cause of any more stress. "I'm sorry. Please, forget I asked. I didn't want to …"

He slowly lifted his head and wiped the tears from his face. "You have a right to ask, and a right to know." He swallowed hard. "I'm just not sure I can tell you anything in any kind of way to make you understand where my mind was at the time. I was a different person back then."

"You don't have to say anything."

Sharon came in the room just as I finished that statement. "Is everything okay in here? Calvin, do you need anything? Or you, Nikki?"

"I'm fine, thank you," I said.

"A glass of water would be great, love."

"I'll be right back." Sharon turned to walk out of the room.

"And, Sharon." She stopped and turned back to face Daddy. "I love you," he said.

She smiled wide and her eyes twinkled. "I love you too."

I tilted my head slightly and took a deep breath. I couldn't remember the last time I'd heard my dad tell my mom he loved her. But it was obvious by the softness and sincerity of his voice there was a lot of love between him and Sharon.

After Sharon brought the glass of water then left again, Daddy took a quick sip. "I owe you an explanation. And it will probably sound really bad. But, Nikki, I was in a different place in my life back then. And there's no way to apologize enough for hurting you and Gary." He took another sip of water.

"I could have never admitted to anyone at the time, but I was an arrogant asshole when I was married to your mother. She deserved a hell of a lot better man than I was. I was all wrong for her."

My mouth fell open at his admission. I had never thought of my father that way until the night Gary and I heard Mom and him arguing. I still, even after knowing everything that happened, wouldn't have been willing to call him that at that time.

"I ran around on her and cheated on her from the time she told me she was pregnant with you." He rubbed his chin. "I don't know why I did it, but I did. I really don't know why she put up with it, but she did. If I had been a real man back then, I would have never done that to her. I should have been faithful or just asked for a divorce. Your mom was a good woman, and she didn't deserve it. And I, over time, brought out the worst in her." He took another sip of water. "Me and my selfish ways."

"So for seventeen years you had cheated on her?"

"Yeah, pretty close to that. I was a real piece of work. You know what's even worse?"

"What?"

"When we got into the argument you and Gary heard, I was an even bigger jerk than I had been up to that time. I tried to blame her. I tried to turn everything around and make it seem like it was all her fault. But it wasn't."

"How did you know Gary and I heard you?"

"Your mother told me. One day, we just so happened to run into each other and, mincing no words, she let me know I had destroyed you both."

"I don't think –"

"No, Nikki, let me take responsibility for what I did. I did ruin our family. Not that day, but seventeen years before that day. And I had been making things worse and worse with each passing day, with each time I slept with a woman who wasn't your mother."

"Did you and Mom talk any more after she told you that?"

"We've seen each other, and been cordial, but we haven't had any deep conversations. Your mom is happy, and she doesn't need me dragging up the past. It serves no purpose. You see, Nikki, what I've come to learn as I've gotten older and matured, is that I really messed up on so many levels. So many." Daddy sat and shook his head slowly from side to side. The tears glided down his cheeks. "I didn't just mess up my life, I messed up your mother's, Gary's, and yours. Do you have any idea how hard that's been to live with these past years?"

He wiped at his tears. "So you see, I couldn't contact you or Gary. I wasn't fit to be a father. I didn't deserve to be your father. And the more time that went by, it just became more and more awkward. Even when you'd reach out to me and ask me to attend something. I felt like I didn't deserve to be part of your life."

My eyes were swollen and blurred by tears. I couldn't believe what I was hearing. I stood from the chair and walked over by the window. I wanted to leave, but we had to get this hashed out. I had to tell him how I felt. "That was really selfish, Daddy. You made a decision for me and Gary without any consideration for our feelings. Maybe, every time I invited you to something, like my high school graduation, it was my way of trying to open communication again. It was my way of saying I wanted a relationship with you." My voice had gotten louder as I strained to talk through my tears. "The way I took it was we weren't important enough to you for you to come see us or call us. Was that it?"

"God, no, Nikki! I would have loved to have talked to you both --"

"Then why didn't you? Don't sit there and tell me that when you know it isn't true." My voiced was getting louder.

"Your actions spoke volumes. You abandoned us to be with your new family. We weren't important to you anymore."

"That's not true. I never felt that way. I never chose Janice and Amanda over you and Gary."

"Yes, Daddy. Yes, you did. As soon as you walked out the door and cut off communication with us, that's exactly what you did. That was our perception of the way you behaved. And our perception was our reality. You did absolutely nothing to make us think anything different."

"I did want to talk to you guys. When I first left I was so embarrassed. I couldn't believe Janice had pretended to be a home buyer, taking the opportunity to berate your mother and tell her about the pregnancy. She knew who Rebekka was and I had asked, no, *told* her to stay away from her. But she didn't listen. I was mortified that happened. I couldn't even imagine how your mom felt, but being the guy I was back then, I cared, but I also didn't care. To me, if I left, I no longer had to deal with any of that."

"So you were a coward. And instead of apologizing to Mom, you kicked her while she was down, and made her feel even worse."

"Yeah, I guess you're right. I took the easy way out of it all. But what I regret the most is walking away from you and Gary. I really wish I could go back in time and change that."

"I can't speak for Gary, but as I've said, I've forgiven you for that. I don't want to live the rest of my life wondering if I should have talked to you, or what could have happened."

"I never stopped loving you two. You have to believe that. I thought staying away from you both was the best thing I could have done at that time."

"Seriously? You really believed that? How could you possibly think that was best for us? I think you doing that had a long-term effect on us both. I think that might be the reason I can't completely trust my own husband."

"I'm not that guy anymore. I know I screwed up. I'm sorry, Nikki. I wish Gary knew how sorry I was too. And please, don't let my mistakes affect your relationship with Jeff. That's not fair to him."

"If I trusted you completely, and you broke my heart, he could do the same to me."

"You're right, he could, but has he done anything to make you think he would? I gave your mom seventeen years of reasons why she shouldn't trust me. And she knew; it didn't all come to the surface that night. We had many heated arguments over my indiscretions. We grew apart. We were only together for the sake of you kids."

After discussing this for so long, I was becoming numb. I didn't like the feeling of not feeling. I had to distance myself from Daddy and take time to think through this day. I looked at my phone and saw it was nearly seven o'clock. "I need to go, Daddy. It's getting late, and I want to see the kids before they go to sleep."

"I understand. I appreciate you coming by. And I hope I answered your question."

"I think you did. I'm not sure anymore." I chuckled, then stood up and slung my purse strap over my shoulder. "I'll give you a call in a couple days, Daddy. It was nice talking to you."

I sat in the car for a few minutes to think. Jeff wasn't like my dad, I was. I had done the same thing to Jeff that Daddy had done to us. I took the coward's way out too. I hated that I was just like him.

Chapter 23

I couldn't help but wish I had gone with Nikki to her father's house. I would have loved to have been a fly on the wall. It was killing me to not know how the visit was going. She was still gone, and I hoped that was a good sign, but I was dying to know for sure.

My phone chimed, alerting me to a new text. I shifted Alexander from one arm to the other, and moved carefully, making sure not to wake Abby. I reached in my pocket and retrieved my phone. Both of them had fallen fast asleep while I sat here, still watching Sponge Bob. Jessica had retreated up to her room, abandoning us, for another night of endless talking to Brad or Chad or whatever his name was.

The text was from Nikki, letting me know she was on her way home. I couldn't wait to see her, and to talk to her. I could only hope she had gotten the answers that would help her understand once and for all that I wasn't going to be the next version of her father.

I really felt bad that she had gone through all of that craziness while she was in high school, and that she thought that her father's actions, somehow, would translate into her future relationships. I had no intention of walking away from her or our kids, though, and she needed to understand that. I couldn't. I loved them all way too much to turn my back on any of them.

I heard keys rattling in the front door, then I heard her footsteps coming closer to me as she walked through the foyer. I looked over the back of the sofa and my eyes met hers. She looked so sad.

"Hey, sorry I'm so late," she said.

"Baby, it's okay. You needed to talk to your father. How did it go?"

"Are they both asleep?" She completely ignored my question. I wasn't going to push her too hard to talk. I knew that when she was ready, she would.

"Yeah, and I'm watching this ridiculous cartoon because the remote is on the table, and I didn't want to wake them."

She chuckled. Not her normal hearty laugh; this was a strained, forced giggle.

"Do you want to talk about how it went with your father?" I asked. I had to ask again; it was killing me.

"Yeah, but let's get the kids up in their beds first."

She kicked off her shoes and padded across the floor, bent down, and picked up Abby. I was able to stand once she was lifted. I turned off the television and lights, then followed Nikki up the stairs with Alexander in my arms.

After getting both kids in bed, we made our way down the hall to our bedroom. I smiled and shook my head as I passed Jessica's room. I could hear her still on the phone with her boyfriend, if that's what he was.

I walked into our bedroom and saw Nikki standing by her dresser, staring off into space, unaware that I was near her.

"Are you okay?" She jumped at the sound of my voice.

"Yeah, yeah, I'm fine."

"I'm not sure I believe you."

"Eh, I'm not sure I even believe myself, honestly."

"What happened?"

"I need to take a shower. Want to join me?"

My cock jumped at the invitation. "Sure."

I stood behind her while she was under the falling water with her back to me, letting it pound into her. My arms wrapped around her body, and she leaned her head back against my chest. That was when I realized she was crying. Her sobs were silent, but her body was shaking. I held her tighter to me, making sure she knew she had my full support. My heart broke for her.

She turned her body and buried her face into my chest; the water lashed against her back. I felt so bad for her. I had no idea what to do or say. I just knew I didn't want to press her to talk about anything she wasn't ready to share.

Her hands snaked up my neck, grasping around me, extending into my hair. She held me tight, then pulled me down until our mouths met.

"I'm so sorry," she said through her tears.

My fingers threaded through her hair, holding her at the nape of her neck, and pulled her into me. I didn't want to talk about apologies or anything like that. I just needed her to feel what I was thinking. I needed her to feel how much I loved her. My tongue searched for her soul, reaching into the depths of her mouth, loving every little bit of her. Her body was saying everything her voice wasn't. She needed me to love her, to cherish her, to protect her, and to let her know she was the most important person in my life.

My hands glided down her sides, down across her hips, and grasped her by her thighs, lifting her until her legs were snugly wrapped around my core. My erection bounced against the soft flesh of her ass. I wanted her so bad, but there was no way I was going to impose myself on her. She'd have to tell me she wanted me.

Her grip around my neck tightened as I pressed her back against the shower wall. Our mouths danced together as the water continued its warm battering on our bodies.

My hands kneaded her delicate ass. Her skin was so soft. Our mouths were locked together. She held me to her with such a tight grip.

She pulled back just enough to talk, but not enough to break all contact. "I want you, baby. I need you to love me," she said.

I inhaled deep, and exhaling into her mouth. I let her back slide down the wall just enough to feel her touch my tip. Tingles ran through me at the thought of having her, feeling her sheath my cock with her sweet, velvet pussy. I lowered her just a little more and could feel her slickness as my cock found its way between her lips. I could have exploded right then with my head surrounded by her.

I let her descend a little more and felt her engulf my head farther in her warmth. I leaned my head back and moaned. She felt so good around me. She clamped her legs tight around my body, pulling me deeper into her. My cock hardened and throbbed, feeling her walls tighten on me.

Her moans filled my mouth and her hips gyrated. She was making love to me, taking me into her deeper and deeper with each of her hip movements. I pulled her onto me, seating myself fully in her. She felt so damn good.

Her fingers tugged and ripped through my hair. "Claim me, Jeff. I need to feel you all over me."

"Damn, baby. You feel so fucking good." I held her tight to me, one hand threaded through her golden locks, securing her lips to mine, the other hand grasping the meatiness of her ass, helping to move her up and down my shaft. It took everything in me not to come.

Nikki tossed her head back and, had it not been for my hand in her hair, she would have slammed her head into the tiles. Instead, it was my knuckles that took the brunt of it.

I moved both hands back to her ass, sliding her back and forth on my cock, feeling her, filling her.

"Do you want to go to the bed?" I asked.

"No, baby, here. Don't stop. Jesus, don't fucking stop."

When I looked at her face, her eyes were closed tight, and tears were somehow squeezing through the corners and down her cheeks.

"Fuck, baby!" she screamed. Her walls clenched tight around me, her teeth bit softly into my shoulder, and her breaths were deep, labored moans as the orgasm tore through her.

I pressed her back against the shower wall, pinning her, and hammered my cock into her tightness. She cried out and pulled my hair. My thrusts were hard and deep. "Damn, girl," I cried out as I sank into her one final time before I found my release inside her.

My eyes stayed shut, my mouth skimmed hers, my throbbing penis stayed buried in her, and my body held her pinned to the wall, preventing her from sliding down. We stayed that way for several minutes, until I felt my softness slide from her. When I opened my eyes, I noticed hers were still closed.

Her eyes opened and she looked at me with an expression I had never seen on her face before.

Chapter 24

 Nikki

"I guess we should clean up," Jeff said. He grabbed a washcloth and the body wash, then set out to wash me. He was so gentle, so caring, and so perfect. He even washed my toes. When he finished with me, he washed himself, then rinsed us both off until there were no more traces of bubbles.

He stepped out of the shower and removed the thick, fluffy white towel from my towel rack and held it open for me to step into. He wrapped it snugly around me and held me tight in his arms for a few minutes, kissing my neck, ear, and cheek. My eyes remained closed as I absorbed every drop of his love.

I turned to face him and was met with his mouth on mine. It was a soft, sensual kiss that said volumes.

"I love you, Jeff. So much." My arms wrapped around his wet, muscular body. "I don't deserve you."

"I love you too, baby doll."

We finished drying and walked into the bedroom to put on clothes to sleep in. "So, you asked how it went," I said. I didn't want to talk about the visit, not really. I was still having a hard time wrapping my head around everything I had seen, smelled, and heard. Mostly, I was stunned by the revelation I had after I got to my car. But I knew if I didn't talk about it, at least say something, I'd never get to sleep. I wasn't sure how much sleep I'd get anyway. "I learned something really disturbing. And to summarize the entire visit, it was eye-opening, disturbing, and I give it an overall rating of *meh*."

"Meh?"

"Yeah. It wasn't good, not bad either, but it was definitely emotionally draining." I sighed. "Daddy …" I paused.

"He had a stroke. Well, he had two. The second one was pretty bad because he's not able to work anymore, and he's in a wheelchair."

"I'm so sorry, baby." Jeff walked over and wrapped his arms around me. My arms instinctively found his waist and hung on tight.

"Thanks. He just looked so different from the last time I saw him. It was hard to take, but I think I did a good job hiding what I was thinking."

"I doubt it. Your emotions are pretty evident in your expressions." He stroked his hands down my hair. "Was your dad happy to see you?"

"Yeah, he was. And I met Sharon, his live-in girlfriend."

"That's good. At least he's not living alone."

"She's not around a lot; she works two jobs to pay the bills. And the house is filthy and smells. She doesn't even have time to clean between work and taking care of my dad." My mind raced back to the foul odor that permeated the house.

I stood and shook my head, my eyes fixed on the floor. "I wanted so bad to ask for the vacuum. It was really bad."

I looked up at Jeff. My eyes hurt and were so tired from all the tears that had already been shed. "I was thinking, just wondering," I said. I stopped. I had meant to check what I had saved in my separate account before talking to Jeff. I thought I had enough.

"What, baby? Just say it."

"Well, I was thinking it would be nice to maybe ask the cleaning people that come here to go over and help Sharon out. I was kind of thinking if they could give the house a good cleaning once, it might be more manageable for her to stay on top of."

"Do you think she'd get offended by the offer?"

"I hope not, but I don't know. Maybe I'll say something to my father and see if I can get him to agree to it first. I just feel so bad for her having to work two jobs and spend so much time taking care of my dad."

"I think it's a nice gesture, even if they don't accept the offer."

My eyes had reverted back to the floor before Jeff finished his sentence.

"I found out something else," I said. I leaned my head to the side and sighed. I was having a hard time wrapping my head around just learning a few short hours ago that I had a little sister. A little sister I knew absolutely nothing about. "I have a little sister. She's twelve. I think that's what Daddy said."

"Wow," Jeff said. "How do you feel about that?"

I shook my head. "Well, Dr. Carrington, I just don't know." I giggled, and Jeff laughed with me. "I guess I feel so many emotions right now -- happy, mad, sad, and excited -- I guess that about sums it up. I knew there was a little brother or sister out there, somewhere, but Gary and I had made a pact when we found out his girlfriend was pregnant that we didn't care about the baby."

Jeff and I sat and talked for a couple more hours. He kept trying to get me to expand on my feelings about my little sister. But honestly, I didn't feel much of anything other than numb. The entire night had taken a toll on me, and the more I talked, the more I didn't want to talk about any of it anymore. Before I knew it, it was nearly midnight and, after we both yawned, we decided it was time to get some sleep.

At two in the morning, we woke to Alexander screaming bloody murder in the next room. I jumped out of bed and ran to his room to get him before he woke Abby and Jessica. By the time I returned to our bedroom, Jeff was standing in the sitting room with his eyes barely open.

"Go ahead back to bed, baby. I'll take care of him. No need for both of us to lose sleep." Alexander was unusually restless. It had been quite a long time since he woke in the middle of the night. I had been amazed at how little time he needed to acclimate to our schedule and began sleeping through the night.

"I'm up now."

Instinctively, I sat on the chaise, removed my top, and held Alexander to my breast. He fidgeted in my arms, wriggling and writhing, but not taking my nipple in his mouth.

"What's wrong with him?"

"I have no idea." I lifted my baby boy so he was lying firmly against my chest and patted his back. He seemed to settle some when he was upright, but he arched his back several times. I set him on my lap and continued to pat his back and noticed his hands pressing toward his mouth. Again, I tried to feed him, but he was so agitated.

"He might have a stomachache," I said. His fussiness reignited, and his little legs kicked furiously as I held him against me.

Jeff walked over and lifted him from my hold and rested Alexander on his chest. As I sat on the lounger in my sleepy haze, I couldn't help but admire my husband. He was so tall, and breathtaking. His pajama shorts hung low on his hips, with that beautiful, prominent V on display, and his muscular chest was exposed. I loved looking at him; he was perfection in my eyes.

"What can we do for him? Anything?"

"Here, lay him down. Then sit on the other end so he doesn't roll off if he starts squirming." We both sat on opposite ends of the chaise. There was barely enough room for Alexander to lie flat between us. I placed a small blanket under his adorable little head and began rubbing his back. He tensed under my hand at first, but after a few circles, he slowly began to relax. Jeff stroked his fingers through Alexander's hair, massaging his scalp. I looked up and saw he had his eyes closed.

"Baby, go to bed. I can take care of him."

Jeff groaned and his eyes opened. He looked sleepier than ever. I felt so bad that he was up when he had to go in to work for a seven o'clock meeting. Even if he went back to bed now, he would still only get another three and a half hours.

"No, I'll stay up with you."

He was a better father than I could have ever imagined he would be. *How did I get so lucky? I was fortunate to find not just one, but two amazing men to father my children*, I thought. I swirled my wrist to relieve the stiffness setting in, and Jeff's hands replaced mine on our baby's back. I leaned forward and rubbed Alexander's head like Jeff had been doing. He was completely still, with the exception of the steady rise and fall of his small back as his breaths went in and out of his lungs.

Jeff reached across Alexander's body, and his fingers feathered down the side of my face. My eyes opened to see him staring at me. "I'm going to put him in bed with us. Then, if he wakes up again, he'll be right next to us," Jeff said.

Chapter 25

When I prepared to walk out of the room the next morning, Nikki and Alexander had taken over the bed. He lay on his back, one foot propped up and resting in the small of her back, the other stretching toward the farthest edge of the bed. Nikki looked magnificent lying there with one arm bent and her hand under her face. Her legs were under the sheet, but they were spread wide, like she had a habit of doing. Her shiny hair covered her face. I gently pushed it back, then kissed her cheek. She never stirred, and was oblivious that our son was using her as his footrest.

As I half-listened to the whirring voices in my first two meetings, my mind was elsewhere. I could have delivered their presentation in my sleep. I needed coffee desperately. I should have stopped to get some before the first meeting, but didn't want to risk walking in late. I had run into more traffic than anticipated and lost the extra ten minutes I had counted on.

My reactions and responses during the first two meetings were delivered on auto-pilot. This job was missing something. The passion I had always felt for my work was fading fast. I was going through the motions, doing, saying, and acting like everyone had come to expect. I loved that I had made it to the senior leadership level, but it still felt like something was just absent. From the outside looking in, someone might think I had gone stark-raving mad for feeling this way. But I wasn't crazy. I wanted something else, something different. I wanted something that would be more challenging and non-repetitive.

My phone vibrated against my waist. When I unclipped and unlocked it, I saw that I had a text from my beautiful wife.

Nikki: *Hi babe, I missed you and didn't get a chance to tell you I love you*

I held the phone just below the conference table and tapped the keys to send her a reply message.

Jeff: *You and Alexander looked too peaceful to disturb. I love you.*

Jeff: *In a meeting, I'll ttyl*

Nikki: *ok*

I wished like hell there was a way I could get out of here for lunch. I'd love to take her somewhere where we could sit and talk. I'd love to know where she normally goes to eat. She had talked about some pizza place on several occasions. One day, I planned to walk in and surprise her while she was sitting there with her co-workers.

****

When I walked into the house, there was a strange feeling. Not bad, just something wasn't like any of the previous days. It was quieter; that might have been it. Abby came running out from the living room, hollered hi, then ran back in before I could say hi back. I kicked off my shoes and walked in to see Jessica sitting on the couch. Abby was curled up to her and they were watching *Sponge Bob*, Abby's favorite cartoon.

"Hey, Jessica," I said. I reached over and grabbed Abby's small body, swinging her into the air. "Hi there, Squirt."

She squealed, and then laughed hysterically. She was laughing so hard she couldn't reply. I set her down, and she gasped to catch her breath, then quickly scrambled to resume her position for that addictive cartoon.

"You're not fair!" she hollered.

"Hey Jeff, you're home early," Jessica replied.

"Yeah, I lucked into an early day today."

She stood and walked into the kitchen. I could tell she had lasagna in the oven, and it smelled delicious. I took her seat next to Abby. I sat there for a few minutes, then tickled her until she begged me to stop. We both laughed so hard. Abby was screaming.

Jessica was on her way back into the room when I stood. "Alexander's asleep?"

"Yes, thank goodness. He's been so fussy all day. He tried so hard to smile, but would just end up crying and screaming."

"Weird. Maybe he needs to go to the doctor."

"Nikki is going to pick up some Anbesol and a gel ring that can be frozen on her way home. That should help."

"Anbe-what?"

"Anbesol. It's a solution to use for babies when they're teething. It helps to take away some of the pain. Or so they say."

"He's getting teeth already?"

"We both think so. If not, the Anbesol won't hurt him. It just isn't the best-tasting stuff around."

"Whatever you guys say; you'd both know more than I would." I walked out of the room to go upstairs. I couldn't wait to change out of my suit.

I decided to work out. Normally, when I would travel, I'd get in a good workout at whichever local gym was affiliated with the hotel. After changing into a pair of shorts and a tank T-shirt, I headed down to the basement.

As I made my way through my circuit, my mind had a flashback to a conversation Hunter and I had a little over five years ago. We discussed how fun we thought it would be to open our own gym. The thought had played out in my mind on numerous occasions, but the urge to explore that possibility as a true reality seemed to be prevalent lately. How hard could it be? I'd need to find a large commercial property and have it designed to our specifications. But that was a problem, as we didn't have a design. Another problem was that Hunter didn't have the funds to go fifty-fifty and help up front. I shook the thought from my mind.

I put on some music and decided to focus on my workout. I couldn't allow myself to keep thinking about the crazy thoughts of owning a gym. While in the middle of my set of squats, I heard a whistle.

"Looking good, baby," Nikki said.

"You would say that." I chuckled at her. She only ever came down here to watch me workout. I had never seen her putting the gym to use. I knew she had worked out after having Alexander; I just was never fortunate enough to have caught her.

"It's the truth. You have a very nice ass."

"I'll never finish if you're going to sexually harass me."

"I wasn't sexually harassing you. I was just stating a fact based on what I see. Now, if you'd like me to harass you …"

"Maybe later, babe. I really need to finish up. If I don't keep going, I might just throw in the towel for the night."

"Don't let me interrupt. I'll go back upstairs. I just wanted to say hi." She walked over and gave me a kiss, smiled at me, then turned on her heels and left.

Chapter 26

By the time Jeff made it downstairs from taking his post-workout shower, Jessica and I had the table set and the lasagna out, ready to serve.

I noticed Jessica had been more quiet than normal. I wasn't sure what was going on. I had asked her, and she insisted everything was fine, but I knew better than that. Her actions and mannerisms were telling a different story. Her boyfriend had called four times in half an hour. That, too, wasn't normal.

Alexander had woke up just before we sat down to eat. I went upstairs to get him from his crib and brought him down to join us. I was willing to experiment with certain table foods, but lasagna wasn't one of them. I was certain he'd love it. Jessica made a delicious lasagna dish, but it was far too spicy, and I was afraid the tomato sauce would be a problem. I was really hoping to get a good night's sleep, and I figured we had a better chance of that if I didn't feed him something that might keep him up all night with a sick tummy.

We were all listening to Abby tell us about her day when I glanced over and saw Jessica with her head down and her fork milling about on her plate. She hadn't taken one bite of food. She didn't appear to even be listening to Abby, which she normally did. Abby finished her story and the table became quiet, except Alexander cooing.

"Is everything okay, Jessica? You're mighty quiet."

"Oh, yeah, I'm fine." She took a drink of her soda pop. "I do have something to tell you all, though." She set her fork down and rocked slowly back and forth.

"I just want to say, I appreciate everything you guys have done for me. I've loved being here." She stopped and swallowed hard. Her hands fiddled with her necklace and moved to rubbing around her neck. "I guess, I just don't want you guys to be upset with me."

"We won't be. Please, just say it." Jeff took the words right out of my mouth. I had a feeling I knew what was coming. She had been scrambling to find things to do around the house lately.

"I loved being here and getting to know you all, but I got a call today. I applied to work at the same casino in Las Vegas as Ben."

"Oh my god! Did you get an interview?" I was so excited that Jessica may have something else already lined up. I had been dragging my feet about having the conversation with Jeff about not keeping Jessica on to help out. I didn't see the reason anymore, and I knew I was more than capable of doing everything around the house and taking care of the kids. I had been talking to the daycare center about taking Alexander, and I knew they had availability.

Jessica perked up at my excitement, and her fear seemed to have subsided. "Better. I got the job!" she screeched. "I had a phone interview last week, and they called me today."

"Congratulations," I said. I was happy for her. And this news was a relief for me. I didn't have to tell her we no longer needed her. I gazed at Jeff. His eyes shifted from me to Jessica, then to Abby, and back to me. The look on his face was impossible to read. I knew he had hoped Jessica would stay, but she really wanted to do something different. Jessica told us she was hoping that by getting a foot in the door, it would lead to a future opportunity to help in the kitchen as a cook, or possibly management.

"Congratulations," Jeff said. "When will you start? And where will you live?"

Jeff

I didn't share the same enthusiasm that Nikki and Jessica did. I could admit it, my reasons were selfish. I enjoyed having Jessica here because I didn't have to worry about the kids if I wanted to steal a few impromptu alone-time minutes with my wife. Her leaving will change that. I also wasn't crazy about Alexander going into day care so young. I had preferred he wait until he was a year old.

"They told me I could start as soon as I get out there. I've been talking to Ben. I'll stay with him at least for a little while, until I can afford my own place."

"You just met him. Are you sure that's a good idea? That doesn't seem weird to you?" I asked.

"I trust him. I don't think he's an axe murderer." She and Nikki laughed. I couldn't wait to see if Nikki would let Abby make this kind of move without questioning her. She's not even my blood daughter, but I'd have a complete fit if she came in the house and told us the same thing Jessica had just said.

We continued talking well after the table was cleared. Our conversation was relocated to the kitchen while the dishes were being loaded into the dishwasher.

Maybe it was just me. Maybe I was just too old-fashioned to comprehend the logic Jessica was using to justify her move; instead, all I saw was the unreasonableness of what she was going to do.

Chapter 27

 Nikki

I found the courage to call my father on my way in to work and asked him about a cleaning service coming in to give Sharon a helping hand. He fussed and balked something terrible. He said no so many times, I surprised myself that I kept pushing him. My last attempt to get him to see how this could help her was an appeal to him to put himself in her shoes. I told him she deserved and needed a helping hand, and I wanted to get it for her.

He complained about the cost and didn't like that I was going to pay for it, but somehow I managed to convince him that I wanted to do this for them both. Eventually, he conceded that she would probably appreciate it, and he made me promise it would only be one time, which I did. He also asked that I come over on the day that the service would be there. I promised that too.

I made it to my desk at the same time Mike arrived. We made our walk to get a morning cup of coffee together. I couldn't help but take him in as he poured his cup full of coffee and topped it off with creamer. My eyes never moved off of him. He was a nicer guy than I had allowed myself to think he might have been. When we first started training, I was upset and disgusted that I was preparing someone to take over my job, but now I wished he was going to be working with me. He was quite bright, and had a great sense of humor.

"What?" He caught me staring before I had a chance to look away. His mouth curled up at the corners into a crooked smile.

"I was just thinking about how much I'll miss you after today. Weird, right?"

"Not really. I'm pretty amazing." We both laughed. "But seriously, I really enjoy this job. My former manager told me I was staying here. But, I've had a great time learning from you. You're an awesome teacher."

"Thank you." I took a sip of my coffee. "I guess we better get back and get Jack's report or we'll both get raked over the coals."

We walked back down to my desk and got Jack's report done and delivered. Jack summoned me into his office, while Mike returned to my desk to get back to work.

"Have you thought about the supervisor position? Are you interested?"

"Oh, yeah, I'm definitely interested."

"Good. This afternoon, I want you to go talk to Human Resources. Then, tomorrow, I'd like you to go begin your side-by-side training with Alicia. She'll show you your new desk, and make sure you learn everything you'll need to know. Once your training is complete, we should be ready to have your promotion go through. Are you excited?"

The smile on my face spread from ear-to-ear. On the inside, I was jumping up and down, and doing cartwheels, and backflips. "Yes, I'm very excited."

"Good, I'm glad that you are. You've earned this promotion, Nikki. I know you'll do great."

"Thank you."

"Now get out of here. I'm sure I'll see you after you come back from HR."

"Thanks again, Jack. I really appreciate this." I stood, turned on my heels, and returned to my desk. I wanted to scream with joy. Instead, I kept my happiness bottled up.

I let Mike do as much as he could on his own. He only stopped to ask me a couple of questions all morning.

We took Mike out to lunch with us. We also managed to convince Tristan and his girlfriend to come along. We had two tables pushed together so there was room for all of us. While we sat around laughing and enjoying our pizza, I noticed Georgia's gaze refocus over my head. I wanted to turn around, but figured she probably was just checking out some hot guy.

In the next moment though, I smelled him, and I knew who was standing behind me before he uttered one word. His hand stroked down my hair, causing my breath to hitch mid-sentence and my eyes to close. My sex spasmed when I heard him speak: "Hi, baby doll." I bit my lower lip. He leaned across my shoulder, and his mouth landed on mine. When I opened my eyes, Georgia was smiling at me.

"Hi, everyone," he said.

"Hey, what brings you by?" I guess there was no coincidence in him asking about the pizza place last night after we went upstairs.

"I was in the neighborhood, and I heard this was a really good pizza place."

"It's the best, baby. I told you it's the best." Everyone laughed.

I introduced my husband to everyone who didn't know him. He grabbed a chair and wedged himself in between Mike and me.

Jeff

Georgia looked up and made eye contact with me as soon as I walked up to the door. I pressed my index finger to my lips, indicating to her not to say a word. I wanted to surprise Nikki. I couldn't believe she didn't dissect my questioning her about this *to die for* pizza place she goes to for lunch.

As I walked over to the table, I saw her laughing and having a good time with her coworkers. She was leaning in toward a blond-haired guy, and had her hand on his shoulder as she spoke. I didn't know who he was, but he'd soon know who I was.

I heard her breath catch in her throat when my hand touched her hair. I claimed her mouth and enjoyed the taste of pizza on her lips. The blond kid didn't even bat an eye.

I wasn't there with the intention of checking up on her, I was just dying to see her. I could stare at her forever and never tire of it. Still not sure of the blonde's intentions, I made sure to move my chair between Nikki and him; my legs straddled her chair.

After Nikki introduced me to Tristan, his girlfriend, and Mike, she kept right on laughing and telling a crazy story about Abby when she was younger. I watched my girl with her excessively animated hand gestures, the wide smile on her face, how she flipped her hair back over her shoulder. She laughed, and it felt like my heart would burst from the angelic sound coming from her throat. I felt like I was in a dream. She was so beautiful and funny and perfect.

"And now we have Alexander, right, babe? Pretty soon we'll have a ton of funny stories to share about him." She placed her hand on my thigh. Her smile widened, and her eyes twinkled at me.

"Oh, yeah. I can't wait to see what all he gets into."

She reached over and held my face by my chin, pulling me closer to her, her pizza breath warm on my face as her mouth closed over mine.

"Aren't you going to eat anything?" Candace asked me.

"Oh, yeah, I'll grab a slice before I head back."

"Nonsense. I'll get it now." Nikki stood and stepped away from the table before I could protest. By the time she returned, I had been drawn into a conversation with Candace about Connor and his commitment phobia.

As Candace asked and prodded about Connor, Nikki cut the pizza into small bites, stabbed one on a fork, and held it up to feed me. This wasn't quite how I had pictured meeting her for lunch to go.

I was distracted between bites, looking at her smooth, toned legs that extended from beneath her skirt. A skirt that I had thought was too short, but I appreciated more than ever right now.

As Nikki raised the fork to feed me another bite, my fingers circled her small wrist, kissing the sensitive underside near the veins, and then removed the fork from her hand. She smiled at me, and understood what I didn't verbalize. Her hand slid up and down my thigh. She was hell-bent on torturing me. My cock began to swell. *She is going to pay for this later*, I thought.

When Nikki glanced at her phone and mentioned their lunch hour was nearly over, everyone except her gathered their things and made their way to the door. She sat beside me for a couple of minutes as she ran her fingers through my hair. "Thanks for coming by; it was such a great surprise to see you." She gave me a quick kiss on my lips.

"Any time, sweetness. I'm glad I came over." I let my hand glide halfway up her thigh and gave her a gentle squeeze.

"Oh, I talked to Jack. I go to HR today and begin my training for the supervisor position tomorrow."

"See, you were worried for nothing. Congratulations."

She leaned in and kissed my cheek while her hand remained twined in my hair. With her other hand, she slid her fingers up my inner thigh, stopping just short of my crotch. My girl was a flirty, dangerous devil.

"Don't start anything you can't finish," I whispered.

"Mmm," she moaned in my ear. "I plan to finish you off later."

Chapter 28

The rest of the week flew by, as did the weekend. We had spent more time talking to Jessica and found out she planned to leave in less than three weeks. She had a lot of packing to do to get ready. We all agreed, though Jeff was reluctant, that Alexander should go to day care during Jessica's last week with us in case he decided he hated it there and someone had to go pick him up.

I had requested Monday off so I could go over to Daddy's house and supervise the cleaning crew. Sharon was at work, and he wasn't able to get around the best. She agreed to let someone come in to clean after Daddy and I convinced her I'd be there while they were. She also agreed to leave the front door unlocked for me. Right after dropping off Abby, I went straight over to their house.

"Daddy?" I kept walking back toward the room we had sat in on my last visit.

"Daddy?" I could hear a faint, low moaning, and a forced cough. When I stepped into the room, I noticed he was leaning over and looked like he was holding his side. "Are you okay?"

"Mmm." He lifted his head slightly, but was still leaning over to the side. I walked around and knelt in front of him.

"Daddy, what's wrong?" His eyes were teary, and he was coughing and smacking his mouth. I saw no saliva at all. I ran into the kitchen to get a glass of water. The first three glasses that I retrieved from the cupboard were all dirty. The fourth was clean. I filled it halfway with water, dug through the drawers, and eventually found a straw. Then I ran back in to my father and pressed the straw up to his lips. "Take a drink, Daddy," I said.

It took him a few seconds to get enough suction to have the water travel all the way up the straw and into his mouth. He began to cough and gasp, then took another drink.

"Thank you." He spoke softly. He attempted to reach out to touch my hand, but he wasn't able to. I set the glass on the floor beside my knee and held both of his hands in mine.

"Do you feel better? What happened?"

His tongue slowly licked out and wet his lips. He smacked his mouth twice. "One of my pills stuck on the roof of my mouth," he whispered. "Sharon was running late and ran out of the house in a hurry this morning. She forgot to leave me a glass of water."

"I'm glad I came by. I hate to think what would have happened."

A tear slid down his face. He pushed himself to sit up straighter. "I don't know."

"I guess it's true, everything happens for a reason," I said. "Have you eaten anything?"

"I ate, thanks."

The doorbell rang. It was when I stood to go answer the door that I noticed my dad had a catheter. "How long have you had that?" I pointed at the half-full bag that was hanging from the side of his wheelchair.

His face flushed, and his eyes lowered to the ground. "Since I came home after the second stroke."

I could sense his embarrassment. I didn't mean to make him feel ashamed, nor did I really want to talk to him about it. I was just curious since I hadn't noticed it before.

After letting in Maria and explaining what all I hoped they'd be able to do in one day, I returned to the room with my father. I convinced him to let me take him out back after he told me there was a ramp for his wheelchair.

The backyard was small and nice. It wasn't overly landscaped, but it was kept neat. I had noticed the front of the house was the same -- neat and kept up, unlike the inside of the house. The backyard had a large willow tree that provided quite a bit of shade. They had a nice small patio set sitting on a cement slab, so I had somewhere to sit while we enjoyed the beautiful day.

The longer we sat outside, the more I noticed my dad fidgeting.

"What's bothering you, today? You can't sit still," I said. He was as antsy as Abby when she had a tummy ache.

"Do you mind going in the house to check on them? And I need to know what time it is. I have a visiting nurse coming by today."

"No problem. I'll be right back."

When I walked in the back door, the smell of various cleaners was prominent. I found Maria in the kitchen. She had brought two other women, whom I hadn't met, with her to help. She wasn't even finished, but the kitchen looked remarkably better already.

"Can I get you anything, Nikki?"

"Oh, no. Daddy was just wondering how things were going in here. He's kind of nervous," I said.

"Please let him know we are taking good care of everything. They will be very happy when we leave."

"I will. And I know they'll be happy. You always do a great job. Thank you for coming by on such short notice. I really appreciate it."

"No problem. I'm happy to help."

I made my way back outside and saw my father holding his head in his hands.

"Something's wrong, isn't it? You aren't anything at all like you were the last time I was here. What's bothering you? Do you hurt somewhere?"

He raised his head, and his eyes found mine. "I'm ..." I watched his protruding Adam's apple bob when he swallowed hard. "I'm fine. Really, I am. I'm just having a bad day today, I think."

"When is the nurse coming?"

"Two thirty."

"It's just after noon now, so she'll be here soon."

****

The nurse came and took care of Daddy's catheter bag, bathed him, and talked to him while I was outside on the phone with Gary.

I spent over an hour begging my brother to change his mind about seeing our father again. He reminded me that it was our father who turned his back on us when we were younger, not the other way around. His feelings were still hurt, and he still harbored a lot of anger. I understood where he was coming from, but I really wanted to try to bring us all back together, at least one more time. I implored Gary, and he finally gave in, telling me he'd only be willing to come to our house this weekend. He refused to go to Daddy's house. I didn't want to meet there, either. I knew it would be too small for everyone. I didn't have the heart to tell him about our younger sister, but I also wanted her to be there on the weekend. It might as well all be brought out at once. I knew it was possible that I would never get Gary to do this again. I just hoped he didn't hate me by the time he and his family left.

Before the nurse left, we talked, and I told her how agitated Daddy had been earlier and that he had been holding his side. She let me know he had a colostomy bag, in addition to the catheter. She thought that may have been why he behaved that way. The bag was on the side he had been holding.

She explained that a lot of times, it was very embarrassing to be confined to a wheelchair and not be able to even tend to bodily functions on your own, no matter what the reason for it. She assured me he was fine, and I just needed to be patient with him.

Chapter 29

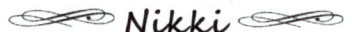 Nikki

I made two phone calls on the way home. The first was to Sky. It was his weekend to have Abby, but I wanted her to be there at least for at least a little while to say hi to my dad, her grandfather. Sky didn't have plans to go visit his mother; instead, he and Hope were going to go to the mall to do some shopping, so he was fine with the change in pick-up time. I invited both of them to come over for lunch, but Sky wasn't sure if they'd be able to or not, and told me he would have to get back to me about that.

My next call was to my wonderful husband.

"Hey, baby, I was beginning to wonder about you. How'd it go today?" Jeff asked.

"It went fine, just another very draining day at the Hollister house."

"Is your dad doing okay?"

"Yeah, he is now. He was acting kind of funny when I was there earlier, but after the nurse visited, he seemed to be in better spirits, and less agitated."

"That's good. Hey, I have to jump off the phone. I have one more meeting. I'll talk to you at home. Okay?"

"Okay. I love you."

"I love you too, doll."

Talking to Jeff, even if it was just for a short time, made my heart happy. I had missed hearing his voice all day.

My mind churned with scenario after scenario about the upcoming weekend. The family reunion. Would Gary really be able to forgive our father and move past everything that happened when we were younger? And we would be meeting our sister for the first time. That would be weird. What if she hated us? Or we hated her?

I tried to push the negative thoughts from my mind and concentrate on what I'd fix for lunch. If I asked Abby, we'd have pizza, again. But I was thinking maybe a Barbeque, with hot dogs and hamburgers, chips, and maybe a salad would be good enough. I didn't want to go overboard and do anything too extravagant. Something light and easy would be perfect.

I pulled into the driveway, parked, and exhaled. *Home.* I rubbed my fingers over my forehead and temples, down my face, turned off the car, and then made my way into the house. It felt so good to be home.

Abby came running to me, screaming with joy. She wrapped her arms around my legs, nearly knocking me over. "You're home, Mommy!"

"I'm home, baby. How was your day?" I lifted her up into my arms.

"Fine." She wrapped her arms around my neck and squeezed me tight before giving me a wet kiss on the cheek.

"How was school?" I pushed her wild hair back from her face.

"Good. I'm smart."

"I know you are." We both giggled. "Where's Alexander?"

"In there." She pointed at the living room. "He's playing."

"Were you playing with him?"

"Yeah." She began kicking and wiggling, so I set her back down. She took off running in the direction she had pointed, and I followed.

"Hey Jessica, how's things going? Getting things situated and worked out?"

"Oh, hey, yeah. I spent some time going through my things to see what I'd be taking and what I'd donate. How did it go at your dad's?"

"It was a long day, I'll say that."

"I'll bet."

"It was very trying at times, but Maria did a fantastic job on the house. It looks a million times better than it did this morning when I got there. Oh, and when I got there, my dad was having some sort of problem swallowing. He said Sharon left in such a hurry she didn't check on him, and he had a pill stuck to the roof of his mouth. Jeez, it was just a crazy day."

"Sounds like it. Are you hungry? I have everything in the refrigerator. I just made some spaghetti and meatballs tonight."

"I'll get something when Jeff gets home. I think I'm going to go take a shower. I'll be back down in a bit."

"Okay, take your time and enjoy." She winked at me. She had a twisted mind and I was imagining what her comment might have meant.

 Jeff

I saw Nikki's car in the driveway, but when I walked in the house, she wasn't downstairs.

"Hey, people," I said as I peeked in the living room.

"Daddy Jeff!" Abby screeched and ran to me. Before she could wrap me in her arms, I scooped her up, lifting her in the air above my head. She squealed and laughed. I lowered her until her feet were inches from touching the floor, then suddenly lifted her again, causing her to let out another ear-piercing shriek. I gave her a hug and had a quick chat with her before setting her back on the ground.

"How's my boy?" I stepped in the room and lifted Alexander. He had scooted across the floor while Abby was away and had been intently reaching and grabbing at the couple of blocks she had sitting on the floor just out of his reach.

"What's new in your world, Jessica?" I asked.

"Just trying to figure out stuff."

"Have you gotten your plane ticket yet?"

"No, not yet. I guess I'll do that on the weekend."

"Don't worry about it. I'll have someone at work get it for you. Do you need anything? Any extra pieces of luggage?"

"I think right now, I have enough. And thank you so much for the ticket. That will be a really big help."

"No problem. Where's Nikki?"

"She went up to take a shower. Sounds like she had a rough day at her dad's."

"I'll go see how she's doing." I kissed Alexander's chubby cheek and set him back down a little closer to the blocks. Abby quickly grabbed them so he couldn't.

I could hear the water still running when I made it to our bed. I tossed my jacket on the bed, then stripped off all of my clothes before walking into the bathroom. I watched her beautiful form in the shower. She must have been deep in thought, she hadn't even noticed I was in the bathroom with her.

I slid the shower door open and she jumped. "Jeez, are you trying to give me a heart attack?"

"Not at all, baby. I need you right here with me. I couldn't live without you, you know that." I kissed her forehead. "What were you thinking about? Usually you know as soon as I step in the room."

"Ughh, it was another one of those emotionally draining days. I'm glad I went over, though."

I took the loofah off the hook and the body wash from the ledge. As she talked, I took my time washing her. She told me about her day, from how she had found her dad in the morning, to their talk while sitting in the backyard, to the nurse coming. But what she was most excited to tell me was how great of a job Maria and the other two ladies had done. How clean the house was and that she wished she could have seen Sharon's face when she walked in. She told me her dad was so happy that he had cried and said he couldn't thank us enough.

When I looked at her face, I saw that she was weeping. I leaned down and kissed one eye, then the other, then skimmed my mouth across hers. "You're an angel, baby."

"No, I'm not. I just wanted to help them a little, that's all."

"Sounds pretty angelic to me, but what do I know." I laughed, and she joined in with her own sweet giggle.

"Jeff, I hope you don't get upset, but I invited Daddy, Sharon, and my sister over this weekend for lunch."

"Why would I be mad?"

"Gary and his family are going to come visit this weekend."

"Okay."

"Well, and I kind of invited Sky and Hope too. It's his weekend to have Abby, and I really want her to be here to say hi to her grandfather."

"See, now you screwed up. Sky and Hope, really?" I was fighting to keep the smile off of my face. When she looked up at me with her apologetic puppy dog eyes, though, I couldn't hold a straight face any longer. I lowered my mouth onto hers, wrapped my arm around her waist and held her to me tight so I could tickle her with my other hand.

God, I loved the sound of her laughing, even if I had to force it out of her. And she wiggled more than either of the kids when I had her in my grasp. I had to hold her even tighter for fear she would hurt herself flailing around.

Chapter 30

 Jeff

I had been nervous the rest of the week in anticipation of this family luncheon. Nikki went shopping and told me what she wanted me to cook on the grill. She was in the kitchen making potato salad, and I heard Jessica say she was going to make cole slaw, and Jell-O for Abby, Alexander, and Gary's little ones.

I had a perfect view of my beautiful wife from out on the patio. I watched her every move as if I were studying for a test. I saw every smile as she talked to Jessica, every flip of her head to toss her hair back out of her face, every kiss she plastered on Abby's and Alexander's faces in between cooking. She seemed so at ease, so calm, but I knew she wasn't. She had told me how on edge she was about meeting her sister for the first time, and how terrified she was that things would go horribly wrong between Gary and her father.

I heard the doorbell ring, and I ran into the house. "I'll get it." I could hear those two laughing at me as I walked into the foyer.

"Gary, Carla, good to see you guys. Come on in."

"How's it going, Jeff? It's been a while, man."

"I know, it's been too long."

"Yep, one of these days, we have to get you guys to come to Orlando," Carla said.

"We're coming to your house next visit, I promise. Maybe we can take the kids to … you know." I may not have been the brightest bulb when it came to kids, but I knew not to say Disney World in front of them.

"They'd love that. We haven't been yet, but someone keeps asking us to take her," Carla said.

"Bianca, Abby's in the kitchen," I told their oldest daughter. She took off into the kitchen, and the two cousins squealed in excitement at the sight of each other. The twins ran as fast as their little legs would take them. Screaming with every step.

"Gary, Carla, oh my God, I'm so happy you guys came," Nikki said. Her eyes welled up, but she managed to hold the tears at bay.

"Like you gave me a choice," Gary said. He poked Nikki in her ribs forcing her to erupt in laughter.

"You had a choice," Nikki said.

"Right, sure I did. Come, or listen to you whine until I said I'd come," Gary replied. He laughed, but we both knew there was some truth to what he said.

"Well, I'm glad you're here. Come on out back with me, and you can help me with the grilling." I reached in the refrigerator and grabbed two beers, then gave a head nod in the direction to the back door.

❧ Nikki ❧

"How have you been, Carla? You look great."

"Thanks. Things are going pretty good. I dropped twenty pounds. I still have a few more to go, but I'm getting there, slowly."

"You look amazing. Oh, shoot, you haven't met Jessica, have you?"

"No, I haven't."

Jessica looked up and smiled at us both. She was holding Alexander so he didn't get trampled by the kid brigade.

"She's been here helping me since just before I had Alexander. Now she's getting ready to move to Las Vegas."

"It's nice to meet you. Are you from Las Vegas?" Carla asked.

"No, I'm from here in Tampa, but I got a job out there after Nikki and me ..." Jessica looked at me, and I shook my head slowly. I didn't want her to say anything about that debacle to Carla or Gary. She continued, "After we did some online research of where some good jobs were."

"Well, hopefully everything works out for you. I wish you the best out there."

"Thank you."

Carla walked over and reached her arms out to Alexander. He smiled and cooed at her, and she swept him up in her arms. "And how are you doing little Mr. Carrington? Nikki, this little boy looks exactly like Jeff, minus the facial hair, of course."

"I know, right? He's such a happy baby, too."

"Well, be grateful for that." She continued to baby talk with Alexander until he was laughing harder than I had heard before. I stood and watched them with a smile on my face, but was interrupted by the doorbell.

Jessica had gotten back to her cole slaw making when I walked into the kitchen with Sky and Hope.

"Jessica and Carla, this is Hope, Sky's girlfriend."

Before anyone had a chance to say their hellos, Sky corrected me and let me know Hope was now his fiancé, not just his girlfriend.

"Congratulations; that's awesome." I said. "When did you pop the question?"

"Last weekend."

"Let's see the ring." I held my hand out toward Hope, and she placed hers in mine. The ring was very nice. We all stood around the kitchen talking before I realized Sky was trying to find a way to escape from the lady banter.

"Jeff and Gary are out back, if you want to join them," I said.

"Sure," he said. He gave Hope a kiss and squeezed her hand. He practically ran outside to be with the guys.

Hope reached for Alexander. He was being passed around between everyone, and he looked like he was loving every minute of it.

We were all having a good time talking and exchanging stories when the doorbell chimed again. I was frozen in place. There was only one more arrival we were expecting – my dad. The bell rang again, but I didn't move. I couldn't move. This was the moment of truth, and I was so scared that what was turning out to be a great day was going to shatter.

Jeff walked inside and gave me a quick kiss on the cheek. He tugged my hand, but didn't hold on, then he went and answered the door. I managed to find the strength to follow behind him.

When Jeff opened the door, I was shocked to see Daddy standing there gripping a walker with white knuckles. I'd had no idea he even used a walker.

I wrapped my arm around Jeff's back, then spoke up before Jeff had a chance to. It had just hit me, I hadn't introduced Jeff to Sharon yet. I knew he was more than capable of introducing himself, but I thought I should do it since I had invited them to our home. "Daddy, Sharon, it's good to see you both. And you must be Amanda. This is my husband, Jeff."

Jeff shook my father's hand, and said hello to both Sharon and Amanda.

"It's so nice to meet you," Sharon said.

"I remember," Daddy grumbled. "How are you doing, son?"

"I'm doing well, sir. Thank you all for coming. Come on in."

Amanda's eyes roamed throughout the house, taking in the entire foyer, then looked back toward the kitchen. "Are you guys, like, rich?" It was so quiet in the house, you could have heard a pin drop. The first words out of this kids mouth was a stupid question like that. I wanted to smack her and tell her that was no way to come into someone's home and greet them. I could use the excuse of being an older sister.

"Amanda, mind your manners, girl," Daddy said.

"I'm sorry." She lowered her eyes to the floor. She didn't seem to like being scolded. I knew that feeling.

"And to answer your question, Amanda, no, we aren't. Maybe a little more fortunate than some others, but we're far from rich."

We all laughed, except Daddy. His face was scrunched up so tight, and he had that *I'm pissed* look I knew all too well on display for all to see.

"Daddy, where's your wheelchair?"

"It's in the car. I'm okay."

"Let me know if you want me to get it for you."

He waved me off and made his way through the house. He stopped at the nearest seat in the kitchen. When he sat down, I noticed the sweat on his forehead. I got him a cold drink of water, then proceeded to introduce him, Sharon, and Amanda to all the adults. I'd planned to introduce the kids when I was able to pull them away from Cartoon Network. Before I finished the introductions, Gary and Sky both stepped into the kitchen from outside.

"Daddy, this is Sky, Abby's father and Hope's fiancé."

Daddy nodded his head and Sky said hello. Then I noticed my father squinting his eyes at Gary.

My dad swallowed hard. His eyes filled with tears. "Gary?"

"Yeah, it's me," Gary scowled. He didn't step any closer to us, choosing to stand near the refrigerator with a beer in his hands.

"Son, that's really you?"

"It's really me." His words were short.

"Oh my …" Daddy lost his battle with his tears. He sat in the chair and bawled. He had been happy to see me, but seeing and talking to Gary; that was completely different. Gary was the oldest, and Daddy's only son. Sharon moved to him and stroked his head and rubbed his back. I grabbed a tissue and handed it to her. Every one of us women were tearing up.

Carla walked over to my dad. "Mr. Hollister?" she said. He looked up at her and blinked his eyes several times.

"I'm Carla. I'm your daughter-in-law. It's great to finally meet you."

"My daughter-in-law. How long?"

"We've been married for over ten years now. And we have three kids. Three of your grandkids." Carla was doing everything in her power to keep from falling apart. Gary stepped over to her and wrapped his arms around her and kissed her cheek.

That was when I noticed something I couldn't remember seeing in a long time. Gary had tears streaming down his face. My big, bad, tough brother was cracking.

My dad reached his arm out toward Gary and held it there. Slowly and hesitantly, Gary reached out to place his hand in Dad's. When he did, he crumbled and fell to the floor at our dad's feet, and cried. His shoulders heaved as he sobbed. My dad leaned his head into Sharon's stomach and wept as his hand stroked through Gary's hair.

Not one person in that room had dry eyes. Even Amanda had tears standing in hers.

"Daddy, what's wrong?" Bianca sat on the floor next to Gary with her legs crossed, her lips turned down, and her little hand rubbing his back. "Don't cry."

"It's okay, Bianca. Daddy's happy. That's all. I'm happy." He sniffled, and I handed him a tissue. "Want to meet someone?"

"Yeah," she said.

"Bianca, this is your grandfather. Can you say hi to him?"

"Hi," she said as she looked up and smiled.

"Bianca, what a beautiful name for a beautiful little girl." He reached out to shake her hand. She sat up and placed her hand in his and smiled wider. He forced a smile to appear on his tear-stained face.

Chapter 31

"What a day," I said. "I think things went really well. Don't you?" Nikki and I were gathering paper plates and cups, stuffing them in the trash can. Sky and Hope had left with Abby shortly after Nikki's dad was able to say hi to her and give her a hug. They were going to take her shopping with them and planned to get her Halloween costume. They planned to take Abby trick or treating this year.

Gary and Carla took their kids to get some ice cream. We had plenty at our house, but I figured he just needed to get out for a few minutes to clear his head. I appreciated the dynamic duo, Brian and Briana, being out of the house so we could finish getting everything back together. Those two toddlers were like a pair of Tasmanian devils whirring through like pint-sized tornadoes.

Jessica had retreated to her bedroom to talk to Ben, again, and my little guy was taking a much-needed nap.

"I think so, better than I had originally thought. I had been preparing myself for a really heated battle between the two of them." She sighed.

I stopped cleaning and watched Nikki for a few minutes. She was stunning. She stood, closed her eyes, then pulled her hair back and twisted a ponytail holder in it to keep it back from her face. My wife, the mother of my child; she was a beautiful person on the inside and out.

"What?" She looked at me with a smile on her face.

"I'm just admiring you, beautiful," I said. I walked over to her and wrapped my hands around her waist. "I love you, Nikki."

"I love you too." I kissed her gently and felt my cock twitch against her.

We finished cleaning up the kitchen, then I held her hand and led her into the living room. We sat on the couch, and I pulled her in close, nestling her up against my body with my arm holding her tight. I felt her head against my chest, and I leaned my head back on the couch.

We sat in silence for several minutes. I was enjoying the peacefulness in the house, other than the occasional laughter coming from Jessica's room. It was going to be weird without her here.

"I need to discuss something with you." I broke our silence. Her head lifted from my chest, and she looked up at me. "I think I need to make a change in my life."

I saw her facial expression change to a look of fear. "Not a change with us, silly," I said. "Have you ever felt like you were just spinning your wheels at your job, and just wanted to do something else? Something you were really passionate about?"

"Yeah, I feel like that, but I don't know what I'd really want to do."

"I know exactly what I want to do. I've been thinking about it for several years and, lately, I can't seem to stop thinking about it."

"What? What is it?" She sat up and pulled her leg underneath her butt.

"I've been thinking a lot about opening a gym. I want to get a big space that I can have free weights, weight machines, cardio equipment, space for exercise classes, and stuff like that."

"That sounds so cool. Would you have a pool?"

"No, that would be too much of a liability, I think."

"It sounds exciting, and it would be a good opportunity. It probably costs a lot of money, though, right? Do you have anyone in mind to do this with or would you do it all by yourself?"

"I've talked to Hunter about it in the past, but I know he didn't have the money to invest up front. If I did it, I'd more than likely end up having to take on the full financial responsibility."

"That's a lot to take on. I don't know, it sounds good, but I'm not sure if now's a good time. Do you think it is?"

"I keep asking myself, if I don't do it now, when would I? I don't want to wait until I'm sixty. By then, I won't care anymore. It's just an idea anyway." What she said did make sense. I wasn't a single man anymore. I had her and Alexander to think about, not to mention Abby. If I quit my job to pursue this, and sunk all my money into this venture and it went belly-up, I'd be devastated that I was responsible for putting my family in that situation.

"It's not a bad idea, Jeff. Do you think you'd really be able to be successful at it? Not that you don't look like you belong in a gym. And what about Hunter? Is he even still interested in doing this?"

"I haven't talked to him recently. I wanted to talk to you first."

"Talk to him, see what he says. We can keep talking. Who knows, maybe my marketing and business education can finally be put to use instead of just wasting away doing updates and running reports."

Chapter 32

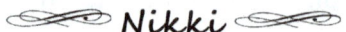
Nikki

I spent the better part of the week thinking about Jeff's idea to open a gym. Of all the ideas for a business, I thought that one had a lot of promise, but it also came with a high price tag. I had done some searching online for commercial spaces and their sale price. It could be done, but it could make things tight for our budget. Once I got the promotion, I knew that would help. At least we didn't have a load of credit card bills.

Jeff had sounded so excited when he first told me about his idea, but by the time we stopped talking, he sounded a little dejected. Now, I was the one excited by his idea. I was the one who wanted to push him to do it. I wanted him to be happy, and just wanted him to be careful, and to make sure that he didn't overdo things financially. We needed a budget and a plan. And we needed Hunter to say he was still interested.

Over the weekend, Jeff gave Jessica her plane ticket, which she was very grateful for. Then Jessica and I went to the mall, and I got her a new luggage set. I had taken a good look at what she was using, and it didn't look like it could have survived TSA's handling. It looked like one good toss and it would have come completely apart. I chuckled as I thought of all her unmentionables strewn about on the conveyor belt on display for all the passengers to see. Little kids grabbing at her items. Everyone would stare at her while she tried to slink back in the crowd, and her face would get redder with each passing minute. It really wasn't funny, but it was.

I was on my way over to visit with my dad after work. I had talked to him on the phone a couple times since they came to lunch, but wanted to visit with him in person and see how he was doing. Sharon was going to be home, as she had the evening off at her second job. I couldn't help but wonder when I'd see my sister again. I wasn't sure what her visitation was like with my dad.

I stood on the porch, and before I rang the bell, Sharon appeared at the door.

"Nikki, hi."

"Hi, Sharon, how are you?"

"Great. It's nice to have an evening off. Come on in." She pushed the door open wide so I could walk in past her.

It was nice to see the house was clean. The carpet looked like she may have just vacuumed. And it still smelled fresh.

"Your father's in the back room. We were talking the other day, and were thinking of getting someone in to look at widening the hallway, if that's even possible. He can get through it in the wheelchair, but there's not much wiggle room. One slightly wrong tug on the wheels and he's banging into the walls."

We both laughed. I looked down and could see black marks on the walls. That explained how they got there.

Sharon took a seat on the couch. I noticed it only had an older crocheted throw across the back of it. No piles of clothes. "Hi, Daddy." I leaned down and gave him a hug. "How are you feeling?"

"I feel pretty good today."

"That's good. Since you're both here, I was wondering if you guys would like to come over for Thanksgiving. Before you answer, I want you to know that Mom will be there, too. And Gary will come back."

My father smiled at Sharon, then shifted his eyes over to me.

"I think that would be wonderful. Thank you for inviting us," Sharon said.

"Great, I'm really excited."

We sat and talked about my kids, and Gary's family for about another hour, then I told them both I had to get home.

"Nikki, come here," Daddy said.

I walked over to him, and he reached out and clasped my hand in his. He looked up at me with a slight grin on his face. He patted my hand with his and just stared at me. "Thank you, Nikki."

"For what?"

"For forgiving me, for allowing me to be part of your life again when I don't deserve to be, for being a better person than I could have ever imagined you'd grow to be, and for being my daughter." A single tear slid from the corner of his eye. "I love you, Nikki. I always have."

I shook my head and tried not to cry. I didn't want to fall apart. "I love you too, Daddy."

"Make sure Gary knows how much I love him, will you?"

"You can tell him on Thanksgiving, but I'll let him know for you." I smiled at him. *Maybe he felt funny saying it to Gary so soon after they began talking again*, I thought.

"Go on, you need to get home to your family. Goodbye, Nikki."

"Bye, Daddy. I'll see you later."

His smile was strained.

****

The night before Jessica was going to leave was extremely hectic. We all sat down in the living room, and I turned off the television. I had been dreading telling Abby that Jessica was leaving. With the hope of shortening the crying, Jeff and I thought it might be better to wait.

"Hey, what happened?" Abby asked. She stood up and began her search for the remote control, which I was holding in my hand.

"Abby, sit down. We need to tell you something." She hopped around a couple of times, then went and sat next to Jessica. Jeff looked up at me and shook his head. I think we both knew this wasn't going to go well.

"Abby, you know how Mommy goes on vacation sometimes?"

"Are you going, Mommy?"

"No, baby, not me, and not Daddy Jeff."

"Who?"

"Jessica is going."

"No!" Abby screeched. She stood up and threw her body into Jessica. "Don't leave me." She wrapped her arms around Jessica's neck and held on tight. "No, Miss Jessi, don't leave." She was crying and making it really difficult for Jessica not to tear up.

I couldn't look at Jeff. I had to figure out how to soothe my hysterical daughter, but I was drawing a blank. "I'm sorry, Abby."

"Miss Jessi, don't leave me," Abby said again, through her sobs. She was beyond inconsolable. "Please!" she screamed.

"Abby, come here," Jeff said. Abby stopped her tantrum and slowly walked over to him.

"Come sit right here by me." He patted the couch next to him, and she crawled up beside him.

"Remember when you went to Las Vegas?"

"Yeah." She sniffled.

"Would you like to go visit again?"

"Yeah." She perked up at the idea.

"That's where Jessica is going to go live. So when we go back to visit, we can go see her. Would you like that?"

"Yeah!" She slid off the couch and landed feet first on the floor, then began hopping about again. "Yeah, yeah, yeah." She hopped over to Jessica. "I'm gonna get to come see you?"

My eyes found Jeff's, and I don't think the smile on my face could have been wider. He was a fantastic father, and I don't think he even realized it.

Jessica pulled Abby down to sit in her lap. "You can come visit me anytime you want, Squirt," Jessica said.

"Jessica, we have a little going away gift for you." I handed her an Amazon box and an envelope.

"You guys have done so much; you didn't need to do this, really."

"We wanted to," Jeff said. "Go ahead, open it."

Jessica ripped at the wrapping on the package.

"What is it?" Abby asked.

"It's a new kindle. Thank you." The smile on Jessica's face was more than worth the time and money we had invested in the gift. She slid her finger under the envelope flap, slowly, ripping the glue loose. She pulled the card out, and when she opened it, bills fell out onto her and Abby.

"Money!" Abby said. She began collecting the bills and handing them to Jessica.

"Oh my gosh, you guys." Her fingers pinched her nose, and her eyes teared. "You didn't have to do this. But thank you both so much." Jessica stood up and gave us each a hug.

Chapter 33

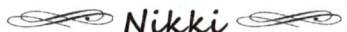

On our way home from taking Jessica to the airport and saying our good-byes, Jeff suggested we stop at IHOP for breakfast. I didn't want to cook, so he got no argument from me.

I hadn't imagined that saying good bye would be so difficult. Jeff and Alexander were the only two who didn't cry; the rest of us shed enough tears to make up for them. Abby was beside herself and begged to go visit right then. Jeff was able to calm her, but she definitely wasn't listening to me.

We sat in the sitting area, waiting for them to call our name. Abby bounced around like nothing had happened. Alexander fell asleep in Jeff's arms. *Lucky baby.*

I retrieved my phone to make sure I hadn't missed any calls or texts. In all of the excitement yesterday, I had forgotten to call my mom, but I'd make sure I called her today. And I needed to make a call to Jeff's mom. Or maybe we could go by and see his mom later in the afternoon.

I dropped my phone back into my purse and threaded my fingers with Jeff's. I glanced at him with a tiny smile on my face. He leaned in to me and kissed my head.

"Carrington," the hostess said.

We stood up, and I called for Abby to come on.

"They didn't call *my* name," she said.

"They called Carrington, baby."

"But my name is Abigail Carmichael. Why didn't they call my name?"

"Jeff gave his last name instead of yours," I said.

"What's the baby's last name?" she asked.

"Carrington."

"And what's your last name, Mommy."

"Mine is Carrington because I'm married to Jeff."

Her little mind was swirling that information around and around. Her eyebrows furrowed, and her lips pursed tight.

We got seated at our booth, and the waitress was immediately there to get things started. "Hi, can I get you guys started with something to drink?"

"Coffee for me, please, and a small glass of milk for her."

"Sir?"

"I'll have coffee, too, and a glass of water."

"I'll be right back with your drinks." Jeff's eyes met mine across the table. I stood and took Alexander from him. I hoped he stayed asleep while we ate.

"How come I'm Carmichael and not Carrington?" There it was. She had processed it enough to realize she didn't have the same last name. A conversation I'd hoped not to have for a few more years, was going to happen now, right here in IHOP.

When I saw our waitress walking around, I wanted to go grab her and pull her over to our table to take our order. I looked over at Jeff, and he raised his eyebrows at me, smiled, and shook his head. I was alone on this one. Alone at sea with no life preserver. Then, as if by a miracle, the waitress appeared at the edge of our table.

"Are you guys ready to order?" I wanted to kiss her. She at least bought me some more time to think about this, but with any luck at all, food would be enough of a distraction that Abby would let this conversation go.

Jeff

I shouldn't have teasingly smiled at Nikki being put on the spot, but I couldn't help myself. Her face was priceless when Abby asked about the last name differences.

She got lucky when our waitress showed back up. I was looking forward to hearing how she would explain this crisis to Abby. But as luck would have it, Abby completely forgot about her inquisition by the time Nikki had gone through nearly half of the menu with her before ordering her a single pancake with strawberry topping.

"Any idea what you want to do today?" I asked.

"I need to call both of our moms. Other than that, I really don't have any ideas. Do you?"

"Let's take a ride to Clearwater. I have something I'd like you to see."

"Okay."

The waitress returned with our food, and I cut Abby's for her. Nikki had her hands full with Alexander, trying to maneuver around him sleeping. We had a seat to put him in so he could sleep, but I hated leaving him on the floor in that thing unless we were at home. She eventually crossed one leg over the other at the knee, and created a little space for him to lay so both of her hands were free.

When we finished eating, we got the kids back in the car and began our drive to Clearwater. I had a surprise for Nikki. A coworker, Hank, had a house that he was trying to sell so he could move closer to Tampa. Knowing how Nikki felt about where we lived, that our house wasn't really ours, but was just mine, I wanted to see what she thought of the area, and what her reaction would be if I suggested we begin a new home search.

As we drove, she called both of our moms. She didn't talk long with either of them, but they were both very happy to hear from her. Rebekka hollered *hi* to me over the speaker. It's a start, I guess. It's really difficult to tell without looking at her face if she was sincere or not.

As we pulled up to the address that I was given, my mouth dropped. Hank never showed me pictures of his house, but just looking at the outside, this was not in the price range I was looking for. This house had to be way over my budget.

I knew we hadn't had any further conversation on the gym idea, but it was on my mind from the time I woke until I'd finally fall asleep at night. Buying a house like this would completely eliminate any possibility of quitting my job and pursuing entrepreneurship.

"Who lives here, babe?"

"This house is for sale. Let's go take a look."

Nikki's mouth hung open at my comment.

Chapter 34

Nikki

I thought Jeff had taken a complete leave of his senses. When he pulled up in the driveway and told me the house was for sale, I was stunned. I had no idea how much that house would cost, but if it was less than two million I'd have been shocked. My mom wasn't the easiest person for him to get along with, but she was a realtor. Certainly she could have shown him some nice places that were more reasonably priced, if he just felt that strongly about a new house.

But, to humor him, we gathered up the kids and walked through. He'd had the realtor meet us there so we could tour the home. And it was a very beautiful, spacious home. There wasn't much that was missing as far as amenities. It had a pool and was less than a block to the beach. With us both working and Alexander being so young, I wasn't sure how much time we'd spend on the beach other than occasional weekends. I did like the thought of having that option, but I knew this house was too much. Every time he'd look at me and smile while we went from room to room, I'd give him a weak smile in return. I wanted to grab his arm and run out the front door.

We thanked the realtor for his time and said we'd be in touch after we had a chance to talk about it.

"So, what'd you think?" he asked me.

"Just tell me one thing. Why? Why would you look at a house like that?"

"It's a coworker's house. He never told me the price, just that he had his house here in Clearwater for sale, so I figured we could take a look. You didn't like it?"

"I loved it, Jeff, but we can't do that. If you still have any thoughts of opening a gym, there's just no way."

"I hadn't realized you were thinking about the gym, still."

"I can't stop thinking about it. Have you talked to Hunter?"

"Oh, yeah, I talked to him. He still wants in if I decide to go forward. He also said he had some money to pitch in to help with the start-up. It's not a lot, but it's something."

"Maybe we should all sit down and talk about that and not worry about looking at a house right now. Our house is fine; we don't have to move."

My phone rang. "Hold on a sec, babe." I answered the phone and put it on speaker.

"Hello?"

"Hi Nikki, its Sharon."

"Oh, hi, Sharon."

"Nikki, I have some bad news. It's your father." I heard her voice crack. It sounded like she was crying.

"What's going on with Daddy, Sharon? Is he okay?"

"He --" she paused briefly -- "he had another stroke. We're at Tampa General."

"Oh my God, we're on our way. What room is he in?"

She provided me the room number, and we hung up. I'd call her when we got closer to the hospital. I couldn't believe this, another stroke? How much could one person take?

 Jeff

After we got in the car, I reached over and held her hand in mine. "It's going to be okay. Try not to get too upset."

She fell to pieces. *Fuck.* I hated seeing her like this. She kept her eyes focused out the window and held my fingers tight in her hand.

"We should be there in about an hour."

"What if he doesn't make it this time?" She sniffled.

"You can't think like that, baby; you have to believe he'll be okay."

It was a somber drive. I knew what she was going through, and I hated that she had to endure that. I just hoped that if this was his time to go, that he could hold on until we got to the hospital and she had a chance to see him. The painful memories of my father dying were flooding my mind, all of those feelings I continued to struggle with were making my heart race. I wished I'd gotten a chance to tell him I loved him one last time. The fact that I didn't haunted me. I shook my head as I drove a little faster.

"Give Sharon a call, baby; we'll be there in about five minutes."

She pressed the redial on the last incoming call and waited four rings for an answer.

"Hello?"

"It's me. Nikki. We'll be there in a few minutes."

"We're in his room. They might not let you bring the kids in, though. Well, maybe Abby, but I don't know if she should really be in here."

"I'm with Nikki, Sharon. I can watch the kids so she can come in."

"Hi, Jeff, sorry, I didn't realize Nikki had me on speaker. That's fine, I --" The phone lost its signal. Nikki called back, but there was no answer.

"No! What the ..." Her breathing was out of control. I was concerned that she'd hyperventilate.

"Relax, Nikki. I'm turning in now."

"Why won't the damn phone call go through? What's going on?"

I glanced down and saw she had zero bars on her phone. "You have no signal; it's not her." I pulled into a parking space, and we entered the hospital at the main entrance where the information desk was.

"You go ahead, if you want to. I'll get up there with these two, and will be in the waiting room." I didn't want Nikki to worry about the kids. I was able to take care of them.

"No, I need you with me."

We made it up to his floor, and Nikki went in the room with Sharon. As expected, they weren't letting either of the kids in the room. I pulled my phone from my pocket and made a phone call.

"Hey, man, what's up?"

"Hunter, I need a huge favor."

"Sure, you name it."

"Is Jackie around?"

"Yeah, she's right here. Why?"

"Remember you guys offered to watch the kids sometime? We really need to take you up on that offer right now. Nikki's dad had another stroke, and he's at General. We just got here, and as long as I have the kids, I can't go in the room with her."

"Aw, man, I'm sorry to hear that. Give us twenty minutes and we'll be there."

"Thanks, man. Tell Jackie thanks too."

Chapter 35

 Jeff

After meeting up with Hunter and Jackie in the lobby and handing off both kids and Alexander's diaper bag, I rushed to get back upstairs so I could go be by Nikki's side. I knew she needed me, and nothing could pry me from being with her right now.

When I went in the room, though, it was empty. There was no sign of Nikki or Sharon. One of the beds was also missing.

"Can I help you, sir?" a nurse asked. Her voice startled me.

"Where's Mr. Hollister? Do you know?"

"Oh, yeah, they took him down to get a CT scan. The two women walked down with him. They should be back soon. You can sit and wait, if you like." The nurse was tidying up the bed tray and the night stand.

"Do you know what's going on? Why was the CT scan ordered?"

"Oh, I can't say. I'm not supposed to comment on that. The doctor would be able to tell you, if you're family. Are you family?"

"I am. I'm his son-in-law." I glanced at her name tag when she stood and turned toward me. "Are you sure you can't tell me anything, Mary Ellen? I just got here, and I really would like to know anything you can share. I know a stroke was what brought him in."

She blushed. "I really shouldn't say anything."

"I promise you, I won't tell a soul."

"I suppose …" She walked over to the door and looked out into the hallway before stepping back into the room. "They're trying to determine the reason for the stroke. His wife told the doctor he had complained of a really bad headache. It was the stroke he had after arriving here that caused them to take him to get the CT scan." Sharon was a clever, smart woman. They wouldn't have told her anything either, if she hadn't lied and said she was his wife.

"He had another stroke?"

"Yeah, poor guy. He's really having a tough time right now. I have to go. I really hope you keep your promise. I don't want to get fired."

"My lips are sealed. Thank you." She smiled at me, then walked out the door. I went and stood near the window, watching the cars below driving around the hospital complex like slot cars on a track.

Nikki

Sharon and I were sitting there, holding Daddy's hands, talking to him about Thanksgiving. I brought it up. I thought it might be enough of a distraction that maybe his headache wouldn't bother him quite as bad. The nurse had come in and given him some Tylenol, but that had been an hour ago, and it still hadn't started to work.

We were in the middle of discussing food. I wanted to know if there were any special side dishes he liked that I didn't know about, or if he had any preference for dessert. In the middle of his sentence, he just stopped talking. Sharon and I both called his name, but he didn't respond. He looked like he had become paralyzed. His eyes remained open, though.

I stood and waved my hand in front of his face, thinking he must have just zoned out on us, but there was still no reaction.

That was when I freaked out and pressed the nurse call button. Within seconds I went into the hallway to get a nurse to come look at him. She came in and checked a couple of things, and then, after a few minutes, she rushed Sharon and me out of the room and made an announcement over the PA system to get some help in the room, stat.

We stood in the hallway for several minutes. It was probably close to twenty-five minutes before the doctor came out to talk to us. We were told Daddy had another stroke, and they were taking him down to get a CT scan. They told us we could walk down to X-rays with them and wait down there, so we gathered our belongings and followed.

It seemed like everyone was moving in slow motion. And I was becoming more and more frustrated that Jeff couldn't be with me. I understood why. I wouldn't have wanted Abby in the room when things became chaotic, but I couldn't help wonder how they would treat me if I was a single mother and had no one to watch her or Alexander. Would they have told me I couldn't go in to see my own father?

I pulled my phone from my purse. I hesitated a moment, but then called Gary. I needed to let him know what was going on. He answered his phone after just two rings.

"Hello?"

"Gary, hey."

"Hey, Sissy. What's new?"

"I'm sitting here in General right now."

"What's going on? Did something happen to you or one of the kids?

"It's Daddy. Sharon called and told me he had a stroke and was brought in. Then, while he was in his room after I got here, he had another one. So now we're sitting down in X-Ray waiting for him to get his CT scan. I just figured I'd call and let you know what was happening."

"Yeah, thanks for calling me. Let me call you back, okay?"

"Yeah, sure. I'll be here." I disconnected from him and held my phone tight in my hand, tapping it against my thigh. It was supposed to be on vibrate, but it wasn't. If Jeff called, I wanted to make sure I didn't miss him.

I looked over and saw Sharon resting her head in her hands, her elbows bent and resting on her knees. "How you holding up, Sharon? Want me to get you anything?"

She lifted her head and looked at me. "No, thank you. I'm fine. I just want them to tell me something. I hate waiting."

"Is this what you had to go through the other times?"

"Yeah, I did. It's just so frustrating to sit here for so long with no information. Even if they just said they had to retake the X-rays, or we want to run some more tests. Just say something!"

My phone rang and I answered before it had a chance to ring a second time.

"Hey, Gary."

"Sorry about that. I'm watching Brian and Briana. Carla went out with Bianca."

"No problem. I was just talking to Sharon."

"When are they going to let you know what's going on?"

"That's a good question. That's what we were just talking about."

"Keep me posted, okay? If he's back in his room tonight, I'll drive over tomorrow morning."

"I will. Oh, I almost forgot, daddy gave me a message for you about a week ago. He wanted me to make sure you knew how much he loved you."

My comment was met with silence.

"Gary, are you still there?"

"Yeah," he said. I heard him sniffle. "I'm here."

"I can let you go, if you want. I'll call back later once we get some answers from the X-rays. Oh, wait, it might take them a week."

I got a chuckle out of him with that statement.

"All right, Sissy. I'll talk to you later. I love you. Tell Dad the same for me. Okay?"

"I'll make sure to tell him. I love you too."

Chapter 36

Sharon and I walked back into Daddy's room, and I saw Jeff sitting in the chair near the nightstand. He had slid down far enough that his head could rest on the back of the chair, and his eyes were closed. I walked over to him quietly, then leaned down and kissed him. His arms wrapped around me, and he pulled me close to him.

"When did you get back up here? And who has the kids?" I asked.

"Jackie and Hunter have the kids. I cashed in the IOU so I could be here with you. And I guess I got here about an hour and a half ago. I talked to one of the nurses, and she let me know you all were down in the X-ray area."

The nurse wheeled Daddy back in the room and repositioned his bed back where it had sat before we went downstairs.

Jeff and I stood and moved back so they had plenty of room to hook up all the monitors and IV.

Daddy was still asleep and he looked very pale. The nurses told us he may not wake back up until morning. He had been given a pretty powerful sedative on top of his medicine. They set his tray table down near his feet and brought a third chair into the room.

Sharon looked exhausted and had a glint of fear in her eyes. Her eyes drooped and her face looked pale.

"Do you have to go to work in the morning?" I asked her.

"I can't go to work. I have to stay here. Trust me, they'll understand; we've been through this and a couple other scares since I've worked with this company. The evening job might not be quite as forgiving."

I leaned my head against Jeff's hard chest and his arms enveloped me.

"Do you need anything? You've been here all day. Have you eaten?" Jeff asked Sharon.

"I ate breakfast before all of this started. I'm not really hungry."

"I could run out and get you and Nikki something and bring it back if you like," Jeff said. "It's not too late to get something decent."

"You don't have to do that, Jeff, but thanks for the offer. That's very kind of you," Sharon said.

"It's not a problem, really. Nikki, what about you?"

"You know me, I'd love some Chick-fil-A if they're still open. If not, Wendy's is fine."

"Perfect. Sharon, are you sure I can't get something for you too?"

"Well, since you're going out, I'll have whatever you get Nikki. Thank you."

Right after Jeff left, Sharon and I each pulled a chair close to the bed and settled in for our vigil.

 *Jeff*

It felt good to get out of the hospital. Being in there brought back a lot of memories that I had wanted to keep buried. I knew I'd be going back shortly, but escaping for a few minutes was like being able to breathe fresh air again.

When I returned with the food a little while later, I saw Nikki and Sharon standing in the hall with their arms around each other, crying. My heart sank. I set their food on the nurses' station counter and ran as fast as I could to them.

"What's going on?" I asked. I wrapped my arms around them both and pulled them close.

Nikki could barely talk through her tears and gasps. "The doctor …" She sniffled and buried her face in my chest.

"He said, it was an aneurysm." Her sobs were louder.

"Nikki, is your father okay? Why are you both in the hall?"

"Another stroke." She choked the words out, then began gasping to catch her breath.

I stood and cradled them both. Sharon was inconsolable. She wasn't able to speak coherently.

When the doctor emerged from the room and walked slowly over to us, I knew the news he was going to deliver was bleak. I could see it on his face. I remembered seeing that same expression right after my dad died. I felt weak looking at him, like my legs were going to give out. But I had to be strong. I had to fight through my own memories and be the strength both my wife and Sharon needed right now.

"You're Calvin Hollister's family?" the doctor asked.

Sharon nodded her head, then managed to reply, "Yes."

"Is Daddy okay? Can we go see him?" Nikki asked.

"Let's go down to the waiting area and talk for a few minutes."

I rubbed my hand down Nikki's hair, then wrapped my arm around her back. We walked down to the waiting room, which was surprisingly empty. We all sat down, and the doctor pulled his chair around so he was facing us.

"There's really no easy way to say this, so I'll just tell you," he said. "The strokes Mr. Hollister's been having are really taking a toll on him. He's not doing well. Based on what I've seen tonight after this last one, he may not regain consciousness."

Sharon covered her face with her hands and just screamed before her sobs took over.

"No, no, no." Nikki kept repeating the word and buried her face in my arm. She looked as if she had gone into shock hearing what the doctor said. The doctor sat before us shaking his head.

"Is there anything else that can be done? Or what are you suggesting?" I asked.

"At this time, we're hoping he makes it through the night, honestly. There really isn't much else we can do. I'm sorry."

He and I sat and listened to the women. They were devastated, and there was nothing either of us could say or do.

"You can come back into the room now."

We all stood up and followed the doctor back down the hall.

Chapter 37

 Jeff

A couple hours later that night, with Nikki on one side of Calvin's bed, and Sharon on the other, I heard the sound of the heart monitor change from a rhythmic beep to a continuous tone. We all knew what that noise meant. The staff rushed into the room, announced for a code blue, and ushered us out of the room so they could try to save him.

The doctor and nurse came out of the room after just a few short minutes and delivered the news. Nikki's dad couldn't be revived. He had passed away. The doctor said it was from complications of the brain aneurysm and the strokes he had suffered, but they planned to do an autopsy for confirmation.

Sharon was devastated and collapsed to the floor, and, if I hadn't had my arm around Nikki, she would have crumpled too. We were at the hospital for nearly an hour after the news was delivered. We spent time in the waiting area while the nurses gathered Calvin's things for Sharon.

Before we left, I suggested I should drive Sharon home, and offered for her to come stay with us for the night so she wouldn't have to be in her house alone, but she insisted she would be fine. She was quite insistent that she wanted to be alone, that she needed that space right now. I wasn't convinced she was fine, but I couldn't force her to accept, and I understood her request for space.

****

Sharon did most of the funeral planning, with Nikki helping with whatever Sharon asked of her. Gary and his family came back for the funeral.

It sucked. Death sucked. It felt like this was draining the life out of our relationship.

Nikki and I had been less talkative since we had come home from the hospital. I knew she had a lot going on in her mind. I remembered going through that with my dad, and how difficult it was. I also expected, at some point, she would open up and begin talking, and I was ready for that when it happened. I welcomed it.

Having Abby and Alexander around provided a much-needed diversion from the somber phone conversations about the arrangements. When Gary and his family arrived, the house erupted with noisy, ecstatic children playing and running about. I caught glimpses of Nikki with a smile on her face as she watched them.

The funeral was small, mostly family, and a few family friends. Calvin had requested to be cremated, so we didn't need to go to a cemetery. Afterward, we all went back to Sharon's house. She had insisted.

 Nikki

I felt like I was walking in a daze. This all seemed so dreamlike. I had been overwhelmed by my own thoughts, and I felt bad that I wasn't able to open up about my feelings with Jeff. I wanted to, but I doubted my ability to communicate them to him in a way that he wouldn't think I had completely lost my mind. But I knew I needed to talk to him about it.

We left Sharon's house after several hours. She had a lot of her family and friends, who were going to stay, including Janice and my little sister, Amanda, but I just wanted to get back to my home and begin working on getting my life back to normal, or as close to normal as I could manage. Gary followed us back to the house. Our drive was very quiet, with the exception of Abby singing and Alexander's little noises.

Jeff reached over and took my hand in his. He had been so wonderful through all of this. I was a very lucky woman. I shifted in my seat, and turned my legs more toward him, then wrapped both of my hands around his before lifting it to my mouth and lightly kissing his knuckles. I closed my eyes and sighed. I loved him so much. I couldn't imagine what Sharon was going through. I had been tossing that idea around in my mind off and on for the past couple of days, and the thought broke my heart every time. I couldn't imagine not having Jeff around, and him not being able to be a part of my life, never being able to see him or talk to him again. The thought of having to go through all of that, if it were Jeff, brought tears to my eyes.

"Hey, baby, are you all right?" Jeff asked.

I just nodded my head. My emotions had caught in my throat and wouldn't let me speak clearly.

I swallowed hard, then cleared my throat, and I was able to speak. "I just love you so much."

"I love you too."

When we arrived at home, we quickly got the kids in the house. Poor Alexander was exhausted and cranky. He had been tossed around between everyone most of the time at Sharon's house and had missed his nap. After getting him changed, I sat down with him and nursed him until he closed his eyes. I walked upstairs with him and got him laid down in his crib, turned the monitor on, and went back down to the living room. Jeff was sitting on the couch, and Abby was stretched out on the floor, half asleep and trying to watch cartoons.

I sat on the couch and snuggled up under his arm. It felt so good to be so close to him. "I keep thinking what if I was in Sharon's shoes. What if something happened to you?" I whispered. I didn't want to talk too loud.

"You can't think like that." He lifted me and sat me on his lap, then pulled me tight against him.

"I just don't think I could go on."

"I think you could. You'd have to. The kids would need you, and you'd have to find a way to be strong for them."

Tears welled in my eyes at the thought. I laid my head on his shoulder and stroked down his face with one of my hands. "I never want to lose you; all I ever want in life is you."

He placed his fingers under my chin and lifted my face until my eyes met his. "You'll never lose me. I'll always be here." He laid his hand on my chest, over my heart. After staring into each other's eyes, he pulled me to him and his lips crushed on mine.

"We aren't promised tomorrow. Let's just plan to take it one day at a time – living life to the fullest, loving each other, and laughing with each other like each day could be our last. Are you with me?"

"I'm with you."

Chapter 38

Nikki

The initial enthusiasm I felt for Thanksgiving had faded after I lost my dad. I had been so excited that our family would have a chance to come together once again. But I guess it just wasn't meant to be.

A week after Daddy had been laid to rest, we all gathered in his lawyer's office for the reading of the will. Much to my surprise, he had left Gary and me each five thousand dollars. Even though I knew it would have helped with the gym start-up, I immediately signed the check over to Sharon. I would have felt guilty for keeping it when I knew she had sacrificed so much, and given so much of herself to take care of my father. Gary did the same thing with his share. She was overwhelmed with relief.

My return to work after the funeral wasn't as difficult as I thought it would have been. It was still a relatively new position, and I had struggled with it during the first week I was there – the week before Daddy died. My promotion resulted in me being moved to the marketing strategies team, where I supervised a small group of four.

Upon my return, I tried to brace myself for an onslaught of questions about my father. Being in a new department was a good thing, given the emotional circumstances I was coping with. Most of the people in my new department knew me, but not very well. They offered me condolences, and said if I needed anything to let them know, but they didn't try to talk to me about what had happened at length, and I was glad, because I wasn't ready for that. Jack was still my manager. He was the only one to engage me in a conversation about Daddy.

I took my coffee breaks and went to lunch with my old teammates on most days.

One week later
Thanksgiving Day

I woke up at five thirty, after tossing and turning most of the night. I decided to get an early start on the potatoes. I had them boiling in a pot on the stove when the doorbell rang.

"Good morning, Mom," I said. She was holding the roasting pan for the turkey.

"Good morning, sweetie. Are you ready for this?"

"I'm ready. I have the potatoes boiling, and the coffee is made. I just hope I didn't forget anything from the supermarket."

"They're open today if we have to run out."

Mom followed me into the kitchen, and we began the turkey preparation. After the turkey was put in the oven, I retrieved two mugs for coffee.

"How many people are you expecting today?" Mom asked.

"Gary and his family, you and Jim, Jeff's mom and Karen, Jims' son's families, Sharon and Amanda said they would come by, and us. If my count is correct, that should be twenty-three people."

"Is anyone bringing casseroles or desserts?"

"Sharon and Amanda are going to bring a pie or two. Carla is going to bring a cake. Everything else is up to us."

I held my mug in both of my hands. My thoughts drifted elsewhere. I had really wanted Daddy to be here. My gaze was fixed on the floor. Then I felt Mom's hand touch mine.

"Are you okay, dear?" she asked.

My eyes met hers. "Yeah, I'm okay."

"You seem a little sad. Is something bothering you?"

"I'm just thinking about Daddy. I'll be okay."

We sat in silence for a few more minutes.

"It sure is quiet. What time do the kids normally get up?" Mom asked.

"Alexander will get up around seven, and Abby normally gets up as soon as she hears him moving around."

My cell phone rang, and I answered it on speaker.

"Hello?"

"Happy Thanksgiving, Nikki," Sharon said.

"Happy Thanksgiving. You're up early."

"I'm driving to pick up Amanda. Do you mind if we come over early?"

"Not at all; you guys can help Mom and me."

"Perfect. We'll see you soon."

Mom and I sat and talked for another forty-five minutes. Our conversation was interrupted by the doorbell. Abby came running down the stairs, and I could hear Alexander fussing up in his crib.

"Morning, Nana," Abby said.

"Good morning, sweetie. How's Nana's little girl?"

"Good."

"Can you get the door, Mom? I'm going to get Alexander."

 Jeff

I couldn't believe I had slept past ten AM. It had been so long since I slept that late. The kitchen was abuzz when I walked downstairs. The aroma made my mouth water.

"Good morning, baby," Nikki said. Everyone else greeted me too.

"Good morning, everyone. Happy Thanksgiving." I walked over and kissed the top of Nikki's head.

Nikki and Rebekka were decorating a cake on one end of the table, while Amanda and Abby were coloring on the other end. Alexander was swinging, and watching everyone.

"When are you going to go get your mom?" Nikki asked.

"I'll leave in about half an hour. Do you need anything when I go out?"

Nikki left her cake decorating to walk over to me and wrapped her arms around my waist. "I have everything I need."

"I feel the same way. I'm so thankful to have you." I leaned down and kissed her forehead.

After getting a cup of coffee and a slice of toast, I left to pick up my mother. As I was walking out, Jim and the rest of his family arrived.

By the time I returned, everyone else was inside. The house was full. Gary and I went into the basement and brought up the card tables and chairs, then set them up around the dining table. I couldn't help but feel a slight pang of regret for having baled on Thanksgiving dinner the year before.

It never had crossed my mind that we didn't have enough dishes for everyone. But Rebekka's foresight was perfect. She had not only brought a roasting pan, but she brought over all of her dishes to make sure we had more than enough.

We all gathered around the table and gave thanks for everyone, and their health. I saw Nikki's eyes well with tears. I leaned in and kissed her cheek. "I love you, baby."

She sniffed. "I love you too."

There was a lot of talking and laughter during dinner. Alexander had a chance to eat a little turkey. He had a couple of teeth that had just come in. He also enjoyed the cornbread and beans.

We said our goodbyes as everyone left later that evening. Gary, Carla, and their family were staying with us for the night. They had the kids in the living room with them. I'm not sure how Gary managed it, but he had commandeered the television to watch football.

Nikki and I were finishing the final touches of the kitchen cleanup when I stood and looked at her. My wife. She was a vision of beauty. Not just physical beauty. I walked over and wrapped my arms around her waist when she stood up. "Thank you."

"For what?"

"For all of this. For being so patient with me. For being such a wonderful wife and mother. For just being you." I lowered my mouth to hers.

"I have a surprise for you."

"Jeff, you didn't need to."

"Yes. Yes, I definitely needed to do this." I reached into my jeans pocket and pulled out an envelope that I knew she'd recognize. "Remember this?"

"Yeah. I do," she said. Her eyes were fixed on the envelope.

The contents of the envelope had been responsible for one of my most embarrassing, and more regrettable blowups. I should have done this a long time ago, but my pride wouldn't allow me to. But I knew, without a doubt, what I was going to do was the right thing, for all of us.

I lifted the envelope in front of me, and with a hand on each end, I ripped it in half. That prenuptial agreement had been terminated. There was no way I would ever adhere to it, so it needed to be rescinded.

"Jeff," she said. Her eyes lifted to mine. A tear slid down my cheek. She lifted her hand and wiped it from my face.

"This was long overdue, baby. I'm so sorry I talked to you that way." I shook my head and sniffed. "And I'm so sorry I put you through that." My arms wrapped around her. "The lawyers have already destroyed their copies."

"You're sure?" she mumbled into my chest.

"Never more sure, baby. Until death do us part, right?" I kissed her forehead. "I love you. Forever."

Epilogue

 Jeff

A year and a half later ...

It seemed so unrealistic when I thought back to where Nikki and I were nearly two years ago, on the brink of disaster, and where we were today.

The fiasco that led to her leaving was a test. If my love needed to be tested so she understood how I felt about her, I had passed with flying colors. I loved her with all my heart.

I always will.

She's a special woman. My special woman. Yeah, she's beautiful, but she's so much more than that. She's a fantastic person, a loving wife, and a doting mother. She's my world.

"Baby, can you get the door, please?" Nikki said. Her hands were full. We were having a birthday party, and everyone was starting to show up, just when the baby decided it was time to eat.

We'd been in the new house for just about a month. We moved from Tampa to Clearwater a few months after I had been laid off from my position and started my own business. I had decided to follow my heart and live out my life's business dream. With my severance and bonus, I bought a huge commercial space, had it redesigned, and it's now one of the top gyms in the area. I brought Hunter in with me. Who better to have help run a fitness center than a man who looked like Mr. Fitness?

"Hey, Jeff," Jackie said. She gave me a hug after she stepped in the house.

"Hi, Jackie, good to see you."

"Where's Nikki hiding?"

"In the kitchen."

"Hey, man, how's it going?" Hunter asked. I closed the door once he crossed the threshold.

"It's going great. I couldn't be happier," I replied. "How are things with you?"

"Great, only six more months."

"Wow, the big day will be here before you know it. Is Jackie driving you crazy with wedding details?"

Hunter rolled his eyes. He didn't need to say any more. "Um … yes." We both laughed.

We took a few steps into the house, but then the doorbell chimed again.

"Baby!" Nikki hollered.

"I got it." I shook my head.

"I'll see you in a few, man," Hunter said. He made his way to the kitchen.

I opened the door to see Rebekka and Jim. A few minutes later, Gary, Carla and their kids arrived.

I made my way back into the kitchen. Everyone was laughing and talking, having a good time. My mother and her caregiver, Karen, made their way down the hall to join us.

"Mom, how are you feeling?" Nikki asked. My mom had not felt well the past two days, but she looked much better today.

"I'm ready to celebrate with the birthday boy. Where is he?"

"He's out back with Abby and Gary's kids."

"I can't believe he's two already," she mumbled. I pulled out a chair and helped her sit next to Nikki.

"Anyone want a tour?" I asked. The only people who had seen the house in its entirety already were Hunter and Jackie.

I gathered up everyone, and we began our walk-through. "Nikki and I fussed back and forth throughout the process, and the builders got quite a few laughs at our expense, but we both are very happy with the end result," I told them as we made our way through the patio doors leading to our backyard.

"We deliberated on the pool since the kids were small, but we decided they wouldn't be small forever. Plus, with Nikki not working now, she's able to come back here with them and enjoy it."

"The house and yard are beautiful," Rebekka said.

"Thank you."

The plans for the house had taken an unexpected, yet welcome turn. What was supposed to have been a six-thousand-five-hundred-square-foot home turned into just shy of ten thousand square feet. Nikki insisted we add a mother-in-law suite for my mom and Karen. Who knew she would surprise me with that request? My heart was near exploding at the thought of having my mom live with us. I think Nikki knew it had been eating at me to not see her as much as I would have liked, and the move would have made visits even less frequent. The thought of not being able to check up on her was causing me a lot of anxiety. Now, I could see her, and she knew if she ever needed me, I was so close she could throw a rock at me to get my attention.

She and Nikki had become very close, and I loved that their relationship was so strong.

We walked through the rest of the house and eventually made our way back into the kitchen.

Alexander came running in, crying hysterically. "Daddy!" He was my boy.

"What's wrong, Son?" I picked him up into my arms. He was an inch shy of three and a half feet already and weighed just under forty pounds. Not a small kid at all.

"Abby did it," he cried.

"Abby did what?"

"Abby pushed me."

Abby walked in just in time to hear him. "I pushed him in the swing. I told him to hold on tight, but he let go. And then he fell."

"It's going to be okay, Alexander. Abby wasn't trying to hurt you; she was helping you swing." I wiped his tears from his face as he sniffed. I turned to Abby. "Maybe just slide now, Abby."

"Fine."

"Where's Buster?" Nikki asked Abby. Nikki and I hated that name, but Abby had insisted that we name our poor little Pomeranian that. He was new, joining the family when we bought the house.

"He's out back with Bianca."

"Baby, I'm going to go get him, and bring him in the house," Nikki said.

I don't know how she stays so calm when the house is full of people. It always makes me so nervous.

❧ Nikki ❧

It was funny watching Jeff juggle everyone in the house. I loved him for everything he did.

"Alexander, go play. Stay off the swings, okay?" I said.

"Kay, Momma." Jeff set him down, and he took off back outside. Abby walked out behind him.

I walked over to Jeff, laid the cloth across his shoulder, and handed him his youngest son, Aiden.

We had been concerned that Aiden would've been born with an arrhythmia, like Alexander had. We were ecstatic when the doctor's told us they no longer heard the murmur during Alexander's six-month check-up, and he's been murmur free ever since. Aiden had been given a clean bill of health in the hospital. We had two perfectly healthy baby boys.

Aiden was another Jeff lookalike at just four months old, except he had sandy blond hair. He was a big boy when he was born, too, weighing ten pounds seven ounces. I envisioned I'd be surrounded by giants when both of the boys made it into their teens.

The doorbell rang as Aiden was situated in Jeff's arms.

"I'll get it," I said. I walked into the foyer and opened the door. Sky and Hope had arrived. They were going to stay for the party, then take Abby for the rest of the weekend.

"Come on in; good to see you guys," I said. I stretched my arms out to take the baby from Hope. Their daughter was nine months old. She was such a cute little girl, and always seemed to have a smile on her face. "Hi, Gracie." She giggled.

"Thanks. Where's the little birthday boy?" Hope asked.

"He's out back with the other kids. I'll get them all in here as soon as the last two guests arrive. Everyone is in the kitchen."

No sooner had the words come out of my mouth, the bell rang. I shifted Gracie to my hip and opened the door. "Sharon, Amanda, hi. Come on in."

Amanda smiled. It was rare that I got to see her. She still went to visit with Sharon on occasion, and just happened to be there this weekend. "How is everything going?" Sharon asked.

"Hectic, but it's going. Come on in. I'm so happy you both were able to make it."

****

The party was awesome. Everyone seemed to enjoy themselves, especially Alexander. He got everything he said he wanted and more.

After everyone left, except Gary's family, Jeff and I began tidying the house back up.

"So, I had a question pop in my head while Alexander was opening his gifts and making a wish," I said.

"What was that?"

"I wondered, if you could make a wish and get anything you wanted from me, what would you wish for?"

"I've always only wanted one thing from you, baby. Everything. I'm your husband. But I also want to be your best friend and your confidant. You and I, we're in this life together, forever. We may have disagreements along the way, but I'll stand beside you one hundred percent, always."

Jeff walked over and pulled me into his arms, then lowered his mouth to mine.

I was his, forever.

About the Author

Desiree was born and raised in Iowa. She married her high school sweetheart and moved to the Philadelphia area after high school and has been happily married for over twenty-five years. She's the mother of two sons and a daughter.

Writing has always been a part of her life. It started as a way to cope with her childhood shyness, allowing her to communicate without talking. Now she talks and writes … and talks. Desiree also enjoys traveling and spending time at the beach.

Twisted by Desire, her debut novel, book 1 in the Lust Desire, and Love Trilogy, was published in December 2014. In March 2015, the sequel, book 2 in the Lust, Desire, and Love Trilogy, *Jaded by Desire*, was released. She has a short story, *Fantasy Come True,* in the Wickedly Exotic Spring Erotic Wonderland box set that benefits the National Autism Association with 100% of the proceeds. And she has a novella, *Unselfish Love*, in the Affairs of the Heart box set.

All of Desiree's buy links and social media contact information can be found on her blog page – www.desireeacox.blogspot.com.

A Note from Desiree

Thank you for reading my trilogy. I hope you enjoyed reading it as much as I enjoyed writing it. I'm honored and humbled that you chose to continue reading Nikki and Jeff's story.

If you did enjoy the book, I'd be forever grateful if you'd be kind enough to leave a review on Amazon and Goodreads for me.

If you'd like to send me direct feedback, please email me at desirecox69@gmail.com or PM me on Facebook. I'd love to hear from you and will respond to each email I receive.

You can also connect and communicate with me through my other social media sites:

Facebook -
https://www.facebook.com/DesireeACoxAuthor?ref=hl

Amazon Author Pages -
http://www.amazon.com/Books-By-Desiree/e/B011OJS8GI/ref=sr_tc_2_0?qid=1447615969&sr=8-2-ent
and

http://www.amazon.com/Desiree-A.-Cox/e/B00QODW54G/ref=sr_ntt_srch_lnk_1?qid=1426635913&sr=8-1

Website –

http://desireeacox.blogspot.com/

Goodreads -

https://www.goodreads.com/author/show/8326258.Desiree_A_Cox

Twitter -

https://twitter.com/DesireeACox

Pinterest -

http://www.pinterest.com/desireecox564/

Google+ -

https://plus.google.com/115253355587352296635/posts?hl=en

Next Up

Look for my short story, *The Ten Year Reunion*, that will be part of the Sensual and Sinful Cravings Anthology.